HONEYMOON

WITHDRAWN

Badenheim 1939 by Aharon Appelfeld
translated by Dalya Bilu
144 PAGES; SC; *391-7; $14.95

The Lonely Years, 1925–1939
by Isaac Babel
translated by A. R. MacAndrew & Max Hayward
432 PAGES; SC; 978-6; $15.95

Sleet by Stig Dagerman
translated by Steven Hartman
240 PAGES; SC; *446-8; $17.95

The Obscene Bird of Night by José Donoso
translated by Hardie St. Martin & Leonard Mades
448 PAGES; SC; *046-2; $19.95

Night of Amber by Sylvie Germain
translated by Christine Donougher
272 PAGES; HC; *090-X; $24.95

**A Love Made Out of Nothing &
Zohara's Journey**
by Barbara Honigmann
translated by John S. Barrett
192 PAGES; SC; *187-6; $16.95

Desert by J. M. G. Le Clézio
Winner of the Nobel Prize for Literature
translated by C. Dickson
360 PAGES; SC; *387-9; $18.95

The Prospector by J. M. G. Le Clézio
Winner of the Nobel Prize for Literature
translated by Carol Marks
352 PAGES; HC; 976-X; $24.95
352 PAGES; SC; *380-1; $16.95

Honeymoon by Patrick Modiano
Winner of the Nobel Prize for Literature
translated by Barbara Wright
128 PAGES; HC; 947-6; $19.95

128 PAGES; SC; *538-3; $16.95

Missing Person by Patrick Modiano
Winner of the Nobel Prize for Literature
translated by Daniel Weissbort
192 PAGES; SC; *281-3; $16.95

Five Women by Robert Musil
translated by Eithne Wilkins & Ernst Kaiser
224 PAGES; SC; *401-8; $16.95

"53 Days" by Georges Perec
translated by Harry Mathews & David Bellos
272 PAGES; HC; *088-8; $24.95

Life A User's Manual by Georges Perec
translated by David Bellos
680 PAGES; SC; *373-9; $22.95

Things: A Story of the Sixties & A Man Asleep
by Georges Perec
translated by David Bellos & Andrew Leak
224 PAGES; SC; *157-4; $16.95

Thoughts of Sorts by Georges Perec
translated by David Bellos
160 PAGES; SC; *362-3; $16.95

Three by Georges Perec
translated by Ian Monk
208 PAGES; SC; *254-6; $16.95

A Void by Georges Perec
translated by Gilbert Adair
304 PAGES; SC; *296-1; $17.95

W, or The Memory of Childhood
by Georges Perec
translated by David Bellos
176 PAGES; SC; *158-2; $17.95

Six Israeli Novellas edited by Gershon Shaked
translated by Dalya Bilu
352 PAGES; HC; *091-8; $27.95
352 PAGES; SC; *199-X; $19.95

Aftershocks by Grete Weil
translated by John S. Barrett
128 PAGES; SC; *282-1; $16.95

Last Trolley from Beethovenstraat
by Grete Weil
translated by John S. Barrett
176 PAGES; HC; *031-4; $22.95

The Forty Days of Musa Dagh by Franz Werfel
translated by Geoffrey Dunlop
revised by James Reidel
936 PAGES; SC; *407-7; $22.95

Pale Blue Ink in a Lady's Hand
by Franz Werfel
translated by James Reidel
144 PAGES; SC; *408-5; $17.95

In the Flesh by Christa Wolf
translated by John S. Barrett
224 PAGES; HC; *267-8; $24.95
224 PAGES; SC; *317-8; $15.95

NB: *The ISBN prefix for titles with an asterisk is 1-56792. The prefix for all others is 0-87923.*

If your bookstore does not carry a particular title, you may order it directly from the publisher by calling 1-800-344-4771, emailing order@godine.com, or by sending prepayment for the price of the books desired, plus $5 postage and handling, to:

DAVID R. GODINE, PUBLISHER
Box 450 • Jaffrey, New Hampshire 03452 • *www.godine.com*

PATRICK MODIANO

HONEYMOON

Translated from the
French by Barbara Wright

Verba Mundi
DAVID R. GODINE, PUBLISHER
Boston

For Robert Gallimard

This is a *Verba Mundi* Book
First U.S. edition published in 1995 by
DAVID R. GODINE, PUBLISHER, INC.
Box 450
Jaffrey, New Hampshire 03452

LIBRARY OF CONGRESS CATALOGING-IN-PUBLICATION DATA
Modiano, Patrick, 1945-
[Voyage de noces. English]
Honeymoon: a novel / by Patrick Modiano;
translated by Barbara Wright.
p.   cm.
ISBN 978-1-56792-538-8
I. Title
PQ2673.03V613 1993
843´.914—dc20 92-39175 CIP

Second softcover printing, 2015
Printed in the United States of America

HONEYMOON

There will be more summer days, but the heat will never again be as oppressive or the streets as empty as they were in Milan that Tuesday. It was the day after the fifteenth of August. I had put my suitcase in the left luggage, and outside the station I hesitated for a moment: no one could walk in the town in that blazing sun. Five in the afternoon. Four hours to wait for the Paris train. I had to find some refuge, and I was drawn to an hotel with an imposing façade in an avenue a few hundred metres from the station.

Its pale marble corridors protected you from the sun, and in the cool of the semi-darkness of the bar you were at the bottom of a well. Today, I see that bar as a well, and the hotel as a gigantic blockhouse, but at that moment I was content to drink a mixture of grenadine and orange juice through a straw. I listened to the barman, whose face I have completely forgotten. He was talking to another customer, and I would be quite incapable of describing that man's appearance or dress. Just one thing about him remains in my memory: his way of punctuating the conversation with a "Mah", which reverberated like the dismal bark of a dog.

A woman had committed suicide in one of the hotel rooms two days before, on the eve of the fifteenth of August. The barman was explaining that they had called an ambulance, but in vain. He had seen the woman in the afternoon. She had come into the bar. She was on her own. After the suicide, the police had questioned him. He hadn't been able to give them many details. A brunette. The hotel manager had been rather relieved because the event had escaped notice as there were so few guests at this time of year. There had been a paragraph, this morning, in the *Corriere della Sera*. A Frenchwoman. What was she doing in Milan in August? They turned to me, as if they expected me to be able to tell them. Then the barman said to me in French:

"People shouldn't come here in August. In Milan, everything's closed in August."

The other agreed, with his dismal "Mah!" And they both turned a reproachful eye on me, to make me fully realize that I had been guilty of an indiscretion, and even worse than an indiscretion, of a rather serious offence, in landing up in Milan in August.

"You can check," the barman told me. "Not a single shop open in Milan today."

I found myself in one of the yellow taxis waiting outside the hotel. Noticing that I was hesitating like a tourist, the driver offered to take me to the Piazza del Duomo.

There was no one in the avenues, and all the shops were shut. I wondered whether the woman they had been talking about just now had also crossed Milan in a yellow taxi before going back to the hotel and killing herself. I don't believe I thought at the time that the sight of that deserted town could have induced her to come to her decision. On the contrary, if I try to find words to convey the impression Milan made on me on that sixteenth of August, the ones that immediately come to mind are: Open City. The city, it seemed to me, was allowing itself a respite, but the noise and bustle would start up again, of that I was sure.

In the Piazza del Duomo, tourists wearing caps were wandering around outside the cathedral, and a big bookshop was lit up at the entrance to the Galleria Vittorio Emanuele. I was the only customer, and I browsed through the books under the brilliant light. Had she come to this bookshop on the eve of the fifteenth of August? I wanted to ask the man sitting behind a desk at the back of the shop, by the art books. But I knew hardly anything about her except that she was a brunette, and French.

I walked down the Galleria Vittorio Emanuele. Every living being in Milan had taken refuge there to escape the sun's deadly rays: children around an ice-cream seller, Japanese and Germans, Italians from the South, visiting the city for the first time. If I had been there three days before, we might perhaps have met in the gallery, that woman and I, and as we were both French we would have spoken to one another.

Still two hours to go before the Paris train. Once again I got into one of the yellow taxis at the rank in the Piazza del Duomo, and gave the driver the name of the hotel. Night was falling. Today, the avenues, the gardens, the trams of that foreign city and the heat that isolates you even more, are for me all linked to that woman's suicide. But at the time, in the taxi, I told myself that it was just an unfortunate coincidence.

The barman was alone. He gave me another grenadine and orange juice.

"Well, satisfied? ... The shops are shut in Milan ..."

I asked him whether the woman had been at the hotel long, the one who, as he rather deferentially put it, "had taken her own life."

"No, no ... Three days before she took her own life ..."

"Where was she from?"

"From Paris. She was going to join some friends on holiday in the South. In Capri ... That's what the police said ... Someone is supposed to be coming from Capri tomorrow to sort out all the problems ..."

To sort out all the problems! What did these lugubrious

words have in common with the azure, the sea grottoes, the summer gaiety that Capri conjured up?

"A very pretty woman . . . She was sitting there . . ."

He pointed to a table, right at the back.

"I gave her the same drink as you . . ."

Time for my train. It was dark outside, but the heat was as stifling as it had been in the middle of the afternoon. I crossed the avenue, my gaze fixed on the monumental façade of the station. In the enormous left-luggage hall I searched all my pockets for the ticket that would enable me to regain possession of my suitcase.

I had bought the *Corriere della Sera*. I wanted to read the paragraph about that woman. She had no doubt arrived from Paris at the platform where I now was, and I was going to make the journey in reverse, five days later . . . What a strange idea to come and commit suicide here, when friends are waiting for you in Capri . . . What had caused her to do it I might never know.

I was back in Milan again last week, but I didn't leave the airport. It wasn't as it had been eighteen years earlier. Yes: eighteen years, I counted them on my fingers. This time I didn't take a yellow taxi to drive me to the Piazza del Duomo and the Galleria Vittorio Emanuele. It was raining, heavy June rain. Barely an hour's wait, and I would board a plane to take me back to Paris.

I was in transit, sitting in a big glazed lounge in Linate. I thought about that day eighteen years before, and for the first time in all those years, the woman who "took her own life" – as the barman had put it – really began to preoccupy me.

I had bought the return air ticket for Milan at random the day before, in a travel agency in the Rue Jouffroy. When I got home I had hidden it at the bottom of one of my suitcases because of Annette, my wife. Milan. I had chosen that destination at random, out of three others: Vienna, Athens, Lisbon. It didn't matter which city. The only problem was to choose a plane leaving at the same time as the one I was supposed to be taking for Rio de Janeiro.

They had come with me to the airport: Annette, Wetzel and Cavanaugh. They were showing signs of the artificial gaiety I had often observed at the start of our expeditions. Personally, I have never liked going away, and that day I liked it even less than usual. I wanted to tell them that we were too old for the profession that can only be described by the antiquated name of "explorer". How much longer would we go on showing our documentary films in the Salle Pleyel or in the provincial cinemas that were becoming fewer all the time? When we were very young we had wanted to follow the example of our elders, but it was already too late for us. There was no more virgin territory to explore.

"Be sure and phone us as soon as you get to Rio . . ." Wetzel had said.

It was to have been a routine expedition: a new documentary I was to make which was to be called, like so many others: *In the footsteps of Colonel Fawcett*, an excuse to film a few villages bordering the Mato Grosso plateau. This time I had decided that I wouldn't be seen in Brazil, but I didn't dare confess it to Annette and the others. They wouldn't have understood. And anyway, Annette was waiting for me to leave, so as to be alone with Cavanaugh.

"Remember us to the crew in Brazil," Cavanaugh said.

He was referring to the film crew who had already left, and were waiting for me on the other side of the Ocean at the Hotel Souza in Rio de Janeiro. Well, they'd have to wait a long time for me . . . After forty-eight hours they would begin to feel vaguely worried. They'd phone Paris. Annette would answer, Cavanaugh would pick up the earpiece. Disappeared, yes, I'd disappeared. Like Colonel Fawcett. But with this difference: I had vanished at the very start of the expedition, which would worry them even more, because they would discover that my seat in the Rio plane hadn't been occupied.

I told them I'd rather they didn't see me into the departure lounge, and I turned round towards their little group with the thought that I would never see them again in my whole life. Wetzel and Cavanaugh still looked very dashing, no doubt because of our profession which wasn't really a profession, but simply a way of pursuing childhood dreams. How much longer would we go on being old young people? They waved goodbye to me. I was moved by Annette. She and I were exactly the same age, and she'd become one of those slightly faded Danish beauties who used to attract me when I was twenty. They were older than I was at that time, and I was grateful for their tender protection.

I waited until they left the building and then made my way towards the boarding gate for the Milan plane. I could have gone straight back to Paris on the sly. But I felt I had to put a distance between them and me first.

*

For a moment, in that transit lounge, I was tempted to leave the airport and follow the same itinerary through the streets of Milan as in the past. But that was pointless. She had come to die here by chance. It was in Paris that I had to pick up her traces.

During the return journey I let myself drift into a state of euphoria such as I hadn't experienced since my first trip to the Pacific Islands when I was twenty-five. There had been many other journeys after that one. Was it the example of Stanley, or Savorgnan de Brazza, of Alain Gerbault, whose exploits I had read of in my childhood? Above all, it was the need to escape. I felt it in me, more violently than ever. There, in the plane taking me back to Paris, I had the impression of having escaped further even than if I had flown, as I should have, to Rio.

*

I know a lot of hotels in suburban Paris, and I had decided to switch regularly. The first in which I took a room was the Dodds Hotel, at the Porte Dorée. There I ran no risk of bumping into Annette. After I had left, Cavanaugh had certainly taken her to his flat in the Avenue Duquesne. Perhaps

7

she hadn't heard of my disappearance right away, because no one – not even Wetzel – knew that she was Cavanaugh's mistress, and the phone must have rung in vain at our place, in the Cité Véron. And then, after a few days of their honeymoon, she would finally have gone back to the Cité Véron where a telegram – I suppose – would be waiting for her: "Rio crew very worried. Jean not on plane 18th. Phone Hotel Souza Rio urgently." And Cavanaugh would have gone to join her at the Cité Véron, to share her distress.

Personally, I don't feel the slightest bit distressed. But elated, highly elated. And I refuse to allow all this to be overdramatized: I'm too old, now. As soon as I run out of cash I shall try to come to an understanding with Annette. A phone call to the Cité Véron wouldn't be wise, because of Cavanaugh's presence. But I shall easily find a way to make a secret date with Annette. And I shall ensure her silence. Up to her, from then on, to discourage anyone who might want to go and look for me. She's clever enough to cover my tracks, and to cover them so successfully that it will be as if I had never existed.

*

It's a fine day today, at the Porte Dorée. But the heat isn't as oppressive and the streets are not as empty as in Milan that day eighteen years ago. Over there, on the other side of the Boulevard Soult and the square with the fountains, groups of tourists are crowding round the entrance to the zoo, and others are going up the steps to the former Colonial Museum. It has played a part in our lives, that museum, which Cavanaugh, Wetzel and I used to visit as children, and the zoo too. There we dreamed of far-off countries, and of expeditions from which there was no return.

And here I am, back at my point of departure. I too, in a few minutes, will buy a ticket to visit the zoo. A few weeks from now there'll probably be a short article in some paper or other announcing the disappearance of Jean B. Annette will follow my instructions and get them to believe that I vanished into thin air during my last trip to Brazil. Time will pass, and I shall appear after Fawcett and Mauffrais in the list of lost explorers. No one will ever guess that I landed up on the outskirts of Paris, and that that was the aim of my journey.

Obituary writers imagine that they can summon up the whole course of a life. But they know nothing. Eighteen years ago, lying on my couchette, I read the paragraph in the *Corriere della Sera*. My heart missed a beat: the woman who had taken her life, as the barman had put it, was somebody I had known. The train stayed in the station in Milan for a long time, and I was so shattered that I wondered whether I oughtn't to leave the carriage and go back to the hotel, as if I still had a chance to see her again.

The *Corriere della Sera* had got her age wrong. She was forty-five. They called her by her maiden name, though she was still married to Rigaud. But who was to know that, apart from Rigaud, me, and a bureaucrat or two? Could they really be blamed for such a mistake, and after all wasn't it more reasonable to give her maiden name, the one she had gone by for the first twenty years of her life?

The hotel barman had said that someone was going to come "to sort out all the problems". Was that Rigaud? As the train began to move, I imagined myself face to face with a Rigaud who would no longer have been the same man that he was six years before, given the circumstances. Would he have recognized me? In the six years since they had crossed my path, Ingrid and he, I hadn't seen him again.

But I had seen Ingrid once in Paris. Without Rigaud.

A silent, moonlit suburb was going slowly by outside the window. I was alone in the compartment. I had only switched on the night-light above my couchette. I would only have had to arrive in Milan three days earlier, and I could have met her in the hotel lobby. I had thought the same thing, that afternoon, in the taxi taking me to the Piazza del Duomo, but I hadn't known then that it was Ingrid.

What would we have talked about? And what if she had pretended not to recognize me? Pretended? But she must already have been feeling so far away from everything that she wouldn't even have noticed me. Or if she had, she would have exchanged a few strictly conventional words with me before leaving me for ever.

*

You can no longer climb the big rock in the zoo, the one they call the Chamois' Rock, by the steps inside it. It's in danger of collapsing, and is enveloped in a kind of net. The cement is cracked in places, revealing the rusty iron rods in the armature. But I was glad to see the giraffes and elephants again. Saturday. A lot of tourists were taking photos. And families who hadn't gone on holiday yet, or who wouldn't be going, were coming into the Vincennes Zoo as if it were a summer resort.

At the moment I'm sitting on a bench facing Lake Daumesnil. Later, I shall go back to the Dodds Hotel, which is very near, in one of those blocks flanking the former Colonial Museum. From my bedroom window I shall look out at the square and the play of the fountains. Could I have imagined, at the time I met Ingrid and Rigaud, that I'd land up here, at the Porte Dorée, after more than twenty years of journeys in far-off countries?

When I got back from Milan that summer, I wanted to find out more about Ingrid's suicide. The phone number she'd given me when I had seen her alone in Paris, for the first and last time, didn't answer. And in any case, she'd told me that she no longer lived with Rigaud. I found another number, the one Rigaud had scribbled down when they had taken me to the station in Saint-Raphaël, six years before. KLÉBER 83–85.

A woman's voice told me "we haven't seen Monsieur Rigaud for a long time." Could I write to him? "If you like, Monsieur. I can't promise he'll get it." So I asked her for the address of KLÉBER 83–85. It was an apartment block in the Rue Spontini. Write to him? But words of condolence didn't seem to me to be right either for Ingrid or for him.

I began to travel. The memory of them faded. I had only met them in passing, her and Rigaud, and we had had only a superficial relationship. It was three years after Ingrid's suicide, one summer night, in Paris where I was on my own – in transit, more precisely: I was just back from Oceania and I was to leave for Rio de Janeiro a few days later – that I once again felt the urge to phone KLÉBER 83–85. I remember that I went into a big hotel in the Rue de Rivoli to make the call. Before giving the operator the number I paced up and down the lobby preparing what I was going to say to Rigaud. I was afraid of becoming speechless with stage fright. But on that occasion, no one answered.

And the years followed one another, and the journeys, and the documentaries screened at the Salle Pleyel and elsewhere, without my mind being particularly occupied by Ingrid and Rigaud. The evening when I had tried one last time to phone Rigaud was a summer evening like this one: the same heat, and a sense of strangeness and solitude, but so diluted in comparison with the feeling I now have ... It was no more than the impression of time standing still that a traveller has between two planes. Cavanaugh and Wetzel were to join me a few days later and we were all three going to leave for Rio. Life was still humming with movement and glorious projects.

*

Just now, before I went back to the hotel, I was surprised to see that the façade of the former Colonial Museum and the fountains in the square were illuminated. Two tourist coaches were parked at the start of the Boulevard Soult. Did the zoo stay open at night just before the fourteenth of July? What on earth could bring tourists to this district at nine in the evening?

I wondered whether Annette would be entertaining all our friends next week, as we did every year on the fourteenth of July, on our big terrace in the Cité Véron. I was almost sure she would: she would need people round her, because of my disappearance. And Cavanaugh would certainly encourage her not to give up this custom.

I walked along the Boulevard Soult. The apartment blocks were silhouetted against the light. Occasionally there was a big patch of sunlight on one of their façades. I noticed some too, from time to time, on the pavements. These contrasts of light and shade in the setting sun, this heat and this deserted boulevard . . . Casablanca. Yes, I was walking down one of those broad avenues in Casablanca. Night fell. The din of the televisions reached me through the open windows. Once again, it was Paris. I went into a phone box and looked in the book for the name: Rigaud. A whole column of Rigauds with their Christian names. But I couldn't remember his.

And yet I felt certain that Rigaud was still alive, somewhere in one of these suburban districts. How many men and women who you imagine are dead or have disappeared live in these apartment blocks that mark the outskirts of Paris . . . I had already spotted two or three, at the Porte Dorée, with a reflection of their past on their face. They could tell you a long story, but they will remain silent to the end, and they are completely indifferent to the fact that the world has forgotten them.

*

In my room at the Dodds Hotel, I was thinking that all sum-mers are alike. The June rains, the dog days, the evenings of the fourteenth of July when we entertained our friends, Ann-ette and I, on the terrace in the Cité Véron . . . But the summer when I met Ingrid and Rigaud was truly of another kind. There had still been lightness in the air.

When was the turning point in my life, after which summers suddenly seemed to me to be different from the ones I had known up to then? It would be difficult to decide. No precise frontier. The summer of Ingrid's suicide in Milan? I hadn't thought it any different from all the others. It's only now, remembering the deserted, sunbaked streets and the stifling heat in the yellow taxi, that I experience in retrospect the same malaise as I do today in Paris in July.

For a long time – and this particular time with greater force than usual – summer has been a season that gives me a sense of emptiness and absence, and takes me back to the past. Is it the too-harsh light, the silence of the streets, those contrasts of the shade and the setting sun, the other evening, on the façades of the buildings in the Boulevard Soult? The past and the present merge in my mind through a phenomenon of superimposition. That's where the malaise must come from. It's a malaise that I don't only feel in a state of solitude, as today, but at all our fourteenth of July parties, on the terrace in the Cité Véron. I can still hear Wetzel or Cavanaugh saying to me: "What is it, Jean, is something the matter? You ought to have a glass of champagne . . ." or Annette would press herself against me, stroke my lips with her finger, and whisper in my ear with her Danish accent: "What are you thinking about, Jeannot? Tell me you still love me?" And I can hear bursts of laughter around us, the murmur of conversation, music.

*

That summer the malaise didn't exist, nor did this strange superimposition of the past on the present. I was twenty. I was returning from Vienna by train, and I'd got off at Saint-Raphaël. Nine in the morning. I wanted to get a bus to Saint-Tropez. Searching one of my jacket pockets, I discovered that all my remaining money had been stolen: three hundred francs. I immediately decided not to ask myself any questions about my future. It was a fine morning, and the heat was as oppressive as it is today, but in those days that didn't bother me.

I had stationed myself just outside Saint-Raphaël, hoping to hitch a lift along the coast road. I waited about half an hour and then a black car stopped. The first thing that struck me was that it was the woman who was driving, and the man was sitting at the back. She leaned out of the open window. She was wearing sunglasses.

"Where are you making for?"

"Saint-Tropez."

She nodded, as a sign that I could get in.

They didn't say a word. I tried to think of something to say, to get the conversation going.

"Are you on holiday?"

"Yes, yes..."

She had answered absent-mindedly. He, on the back seat, was studying a map that was much bigger than the Michelin maps. I could see him clearly, in the rear-view mirror.

"We're just coming to Les Issambres."

She looked at the signs on the side of the road. Then she turned her face to me:

"Would you mind if we stopped for a moment at Les Issambres?"

She said this quite naturally, as if we'd known each other for a long time.

"We'll stop, but then we'll go on to Saint-Tropez," he told me with a smile.

He had folded his map and put it down beside him on the seat. I reckoned they were both about thirty-five. She was dark, and had light eyes. He had short hair brushed back, a massive face and a slightly squashed nose. He was wearing a suede jacket.

"This must be it ... The chap's waiting for us ..."

He leaned over towards her and put his hand on her shoulder. A man in a summer suit, carrying a heavy black briefcase, was pacing up and down in front of the iron gate outside a villa. She parked the car on the pavement, a few metres away from the gate.

"We'll only be a moment," she said. "Can you wait for us in the car?"

He got out first, and went and opened the door for her. When she was out, he shut the door himself. Then he put his head through the open window.

"If you get bored, you can have a cigarette ... There's a packet in the glove compartment..."

They walked up to the man with the briefcase. I noticed that he had a slight limp, but he held himself very straight, and put his arm round her shoulder with a protective gesture. They shook hands with the man with the briefcase, who opened the gate and let them precede him.

*

Looking for the packet of cigarettes in the glove compartment, I knocked a passport out of it. Before I put it back, I opened it: I couldn't say whether I did so automatically or whether I was prompted by simple curiosity. A French passport in the name of Ingrid Teyrsen, married name Rigaud. What surprised me was that she had been born in Austria, in Vienna, the town I'd been living in for a few months. I lit a cigarette, but the very first puff made me feel sick. I had spent a sleepless night in the train, and I hadn't eaten since lunch the previous day.

I didn't get out of the car. I tried to ward off my exhaustion, but every now and then I fell into a kind of doze. I heard the murmur of a conversation and opened my eyes: they were standing near the car with the man with the black briefcase. They shook hands, and he strode off across the avenue.

I opened the door and got out of the car.

"Wouldn't you like to sit in front?" I asked the man.

"No ... no ... I have to sit in the back because of my leg ... I still can't quite bend it ... An old injury to my knee ..."

It was almost as if he was trying to reassure me. He smiled at me. Was he the Rigaud mentioned in the passport?

"You can get in," she said to me with a charming frown.

She opened the glove compartment and took a cigarette. She drove off with a slight jerk. He was sitting sideways on the back seat, with one of his legs resting on it.

*

She drove slowly, and I had difficulty in keeping my eyes open.

"Are you on holiday?" she asked me.

I was afraid they would ask me other, more precise questions: What's your address? Are you a student?

"Not really on holiday," I said. "I'm not quite sure whether I'll stay here."

"We live in a little house near Pampelonne beach," she told me. "But we're looking for something else to rent ... While you were waiting for us we were visiting a villa ... It's a pity ... I find it too big ..."

Behind us, he remained silent. He was massaging his knee with one hand.

"What *I* liked was the name: Les Issambres . . . Don't you think that's a nice name?"

And she looked at me from behind her sunglasses.

*

At the entrance to Saint-Tropez we turned right and took the road along the beaches.

"From here on, I always take the wrong road," she said.

"You go straight on."

He spoke in a low voice, with a slight Paris accent, which gave me the idea of asking them whether they lived in Paris.

"Yes, but we may come and live here for good," she said.

"And you, do you live in Paris?"

I turned round towards him. His leg was still lying across the seat. I had the impression that he was giving me an ironical look.

"Yes. I live in Paris."

"With your parents?"

"No."

"Leave him alone," she said. "We aren't the police."

The sea appeared in the background, slightly below the road, beyond an expanse of vines and pines.

"You've gone too far again," he said. "You should have turned left."

She made a U-turn, and only just avoided a car coming in the opposite direction.

"Aren't you frightened?" he asked me. "Ingrid is a very bad driver. In a few days, when my leg's better, I'll be able to drive again."

We had turned into a little road at the beginning of which was a signpost: TAHITI-MOOREA.

"Have you got a driving licence?" she asked me.

"Yes."

"Then you can drive instead of me. It'd be wiser."

She stopped at a crossroads, and I was getting ready to take her place at the wheel when she said:

"No ... no ... Not right away ... Later ..."

"It's on the left," he told her.

And he pointed to another signpost: TAHITI-MOOREA

*

The road was now nothing but a track bordered by reeds. We had driven round a wall with a navy-blue door in it. She stopped the car outside the door.

"I'd rather go home by the beach," he said.

We continued along the reed track and came to a piece of ground used as a car park for the Moorea restaurant. We parked the car and then crossed the deserted terrace of the restaurant. We were on the beach.

"It's a bit farther on," he said. "We can walk there ..."

She had removed her espadrilles and taken his arm. He still limped, but in a less pronounced fashion than before.

"There's no one on the beach yet," she said to me. "This is the time of day I like best."

The property was separated from the beach by a wire fence with holes in it. We slid through one of the holes. About fifty metres farther on there was a bungalow which reminded me of the motels on American expressways. It was in the shade of a little pinewood.

"The main villa is over there," he told me.

In the background I could make out, through the pines, a big, white one-storey building in the Moorish or Spanish style, which surrounded a swimming pool with blue mosaics. Someone was bathing in the pool.

"The owners live there," he told me. "We rented their gardener's house from them."

*

She came out of the bungalow in a sky-blue swimming costume. We had waited for her, he and I, sitting on the deck chairs in front of the sliding glass doors.

"You look tired," he said. "You can rest here. We're going down to the beach ... just in front..."

She looked at me in silence, from behind her dark glasses. Then she said:

"You ought to have a siesta."

And she pointed to a big pneumatic mattress at the foot of a clump of pines by the side of the bungalow.

*

I was lying on the mattress, staring at the sky and the top of the pines. I could hear shouts coming from the swimming pool, down below, and the sound of people diving. Above me, between the branches, the play of sun and shade. I let myself sink into a delightful torpor. Remembering it now, it seems to me that that was one of the rare moments in my life when I experienced a sense of well-being that I could even call Happiness. In that semi-somnolent state, occasionally interrupted by a shaft of sunlight piercing the shade of the pines and dazzling me, I considered it perfectly natural that they had taken me home with them, as if we had known each other for a long time. In any case, I had no choice. I'd just have to wait and see how things would go. I finally fell asleep.

*

I could hear them talking by my side, but I couldn't open my eyes. An orange light was filtering through my eyelids. I felt the pressure of a hand on my shoulder.

"Well? Have a good sleep?"

I sat up abruptly. He was wearing linen trousers, a black polo-neck, and sunglasses. And she, a bath robe. Her hair was wet. She must have just been bathing.

"It's nearly three o'clock," he said. "Will you have lunch with us?"

"I don't want to impose upon you."

I was still half asleep.

"But you won't be imposing upon us in the least ... Will he, Ingrid?"

"Not in the least."

She smiled, and looked intently at me with her pale blue or grey eyes.

We walked along the beach to the terrace of the Moorea restaurant. Most of the tables were empty. We sat down at the one that was protected from the sun by a green sun umbrella. A man with the physique of a former ski instructor came to take our order.

"The usual," she said. "For three."

*

The sun enveloped the beach, the sea, and the Moorea terrace in a sheet of silence. And against this background of silence, the slightest sound stood out with unusual acuity: the voices of a group of people in swimming costumes at a table some way away from ours, whose conversation we could follow as if they were sitting next to us; the drone of a Chriscraft gliding over the calm sea and from time to time letting itself float, its engine switched off. And then we heard the laughter and shouts of the people on board.

"If I understand rightly," he said to me, "you weren't making for anywhere in particular."

"No."

"You were just drifting..."

Not the slightest irony in his voice. On the contrary, I detected fellow-feeling in it.

"But unfortunately, I have to get back to Paris as soon as possible for my work."

"What kind of work?"

This time it was she who was questioning me, her pale eyes still fixed on me.

"I write articles for geographical magazines . . ."

I was only half lying. I had written a long article on the journalist and explorer Henry M. Stanley and sent it to a travel magazine, but I still didn't know whether it would be published.

"And you've just come back from a trip?" he asked.

"Yes. From Austria. Vienna."

I was hoping to steer the conversation round to Vienna. She ought to know it well, seeing that she had been born there. To my great astonishment, she didn't react.

"It's a very beautiful city, Vienna."

It was no use my insisting. Vienna didn't mean a thing to her.

"And you, do you work in Paris?"

"I've retired," he answered with a smile, but in an abrupt tone which discouraged further questions.

"I'm going to bathe. Will you wait here for me?"

She stood up and took off her white bath robe. I watched her in the heat haze. She crossed the beach, then walked into the sea, and when the water came up to her waist she began to swim on her back.

*

We met again in the shade of the pines by the bungalow. We played a game of cards they taught me whose rules were very simple. That was the only time in my life that I have played cards. And then we got to the end of the afternoon.

"I'm going to do a bit of shopping," she said.

He turned towards me:

"Could you go with her? It'd be wiser . . . She hasn't got a driving licence . . . I didn't want to tell you, earlier . . . You might have been afraid we'd be stopped on the Saint-Raphaël road . . ."

He gave a short little laugh.

"I'm not afraid of anything," I told him.

"You're right . . . Nor were we, either, at your age . . ."

"But we're still not afraid of anything," she said, raising her index finger.

*

I always kept my passport and driving licence in the inside pocket of my jacket. I sat at the wheel. I had trouble in moving off and getting out of the Moorea car park, because I hadn't driven for some time.

"I have a feeling that you drive even worse than I do," she said.

She showed me the way. Once again the little track bordered by bamboos. It was so narrow that every time a car came in the opposite direction I had to pull in on to the verge.

"Would you like me to take over?" she asked.

"No, no. It'll be quite all right."

*

I parked the car outside the Hôtel de Paris, whose façade and little windows with their wooden shutters made it look like an hotel in the mountains, and we walked down to the port. It was the time of day when groups of tourists were strolling along the quayside admiring the moored yachts, or trying to find a free table on the terrace of Senéquier's. She bought a few things at the chemist's. She asked me whether I needed anything, and after a moment's hesitation I confessed that I needed some Extra Blue Gillette razor blades and some shaving cream, but that I hadn't any money on me. Then we went to the bookshop where she picked out a detective story. Next, to the port's *bar-tabac*. She bought a few packets of cigarettes. We had difficulty in making our way through the crowd.

A little later, though, we were the only ones walking through the alleyways in the old town. I went back to that place in the course of the following years, and walked along the port and the same little streets with Annette, Wetzel and Cavanaugh. I couldn't help it, I couldn't entirely share their lightheartedness and *joie de vivre*. I was somewhere else, in another summer, more and more distant, and with time the light of that summer underwent a curious transformation: far from fading, like old, over-exposed photos, the contrasts of sun and shade became so accentuated that I recall everything in black and white.

We walked down the Rue de la Ponche, and when we'd passed the arch we stopped in the square overlooking the Port des Pêcheurs. She pointed to the terrace of a derelict house.

"My husband and I used to live up there, a very long time ago ... You were't even born ..."

Her pale eyes were still fixed on me, with their absent expression which intimidated me. But she was frowning in the way I had already noticed, which made her look as if she was gently mocking me.

"How about a little stroll?"

In the sloping garden at the foot of the Citadelle, we sat down on a bench.

"Have you parents?"

"I don't see them any more," I told her.

"Why not?"

That frown again. What could I answer? Strange sort of parents, who had always tried to find a boarding school or reformatory where they could get rid of me.

"When I saw you by the side of the road this morning, I wondered whether you had parents."

We went back to the port down the Rue de la Citadelle.

She took my arm because of the sloping road. The contact of her arm and shoulder gave me an impression I had never yet had, that of finding myself under someone's protection. She would be the first person who could help me. I felt light-headed. All those waves of tenderness that she communicated to me through the simple contact of her arm, and the pale blue look she gave me from time to time – I didn't know that such things could happen, in life.

*

We had come back to the bungalow along the beach. We were sitting in the deck chairs. Night had fallen, and the light from the bungalow was shining on us through one of the glass doors.

"A game of cards?" he said. "But you don't seem all that keen on such activities . . ."

"Did *we* play cards at his age?"

She called him to witness, and he smiled.

"We didn't have time to play cards."

He had said this in a low voice, for himself alone, and I would have been curious to know what they had done for a living at that time.

"You can stay the night here, if you have nowhere else to go," she said.

I was ashamed at the idea that they took me for a tramp.

"Thank you . . . I'd like to, if it's not too much of an imposition . . ."

It was difficult to say, and I dug my nails into the palms of my hands to give myself courage. But the worst thing still remained to be confessed:

"I've got to go back to Paris tomorrow. Unfortunately, all my remaining money was stolen."

Rather than hang my head, I looked her straight in the eyes, waiting for her verdict. Once again, she frowned.

"And that bothers you?"

"Don't worry," he said. "We'll find you a seat on the train tomorrow."

Above us, behind the pines, the villa and its swimming pool were lit up, and I could see silhouettes gliding over the blue mosaic.

"They have parties every night," he said. "They stop us sleeping. That's why we're looking for another house."

He suddenly looked worn out.

"At the beginning, they were always inviting us to their parties," she said. "So we used to turn out all the lights in the bungalow and pretend we weren't there."

"We'd sit in the dark. One evening they came down to fetch us. We took refuge under the pines, over there..."

Why were they adopting this confidential, or even confessional tone with me, as if they were trying to justify themselves?

"Do you know them?" I asked.

"Yes, yes, a little," he said. "But we don't want to see them..."

"We've become savages," she said.

Voices were approaching. A little group, about fifty metres away, was coming along the pine-bordered path.

"Do you mind if we put the light out?" he asked me.

He went into the bungalow and the light went out, leaving us, her and me, in the semi-darkness. She put her hand on my wrist.

"Now," she said, "we must talk very quietly."

And she smiled at me. Behind us, he shut the sliding glass door slowly, so as not to make a noise, and came and sat down on the deck chair again. The others were very close now, just by the path leading to the bungalow. I heard one of them keep repeating in a husky voice:

"But I swear I did! I swear I did..."

"If they come right up to us, we'll just have to pretend to be asleep," he said.

I thought of the curious sight we should present to them, asleep on our deck chairs in the dark.

"And if they tap us on the shoulder to wake us up?" I asked.

"Well, in that case we'll pretend to be dead," she said.

But they left the bungalow path and went down the slope under the pines in the direction of the beach. In the moonlight, I could make out two men and three women.

"The danger's over," he said. "We'd better stay in the dark. They might quite likely see the light from the beach."

I didn't know whether it was a game or whether he was in earnest.

"Does our attitude surprise you?" she asked me, in a gentle voice. "There are moments when we are incapable of exchanging a single word with anybody ... It's beyond us ..."

Their silhouettes could be seen on the beach. They took off their clothes and put them down on a big tree trunk carved into the shape of a Polynesian totem pole, whose shadow gave you the impression of being on the shore of a lagoon, somewhere in the South Seas. The women, stark naked, ran down to the sea. The men pretended to chase them, uttering roars. Snatches of music and the hum of conversation came from the villa in the background.

"It lasts until three in the morning," he said in a weary voice. "They dance and go for midnight bathes."

For several moments we remained silent, in our deck chairs, in the dark, as if we were hiding.

*

It was she who woke me. When I opened my eyes I saw that pale blue or grey gaze fixed on me once again. She opened the sliding glass door of the bedroom and the morning sunshine dazzled me. We all three had breakfast outside. The scent of the pines was floating around us. Down below, the beach was deserted. No trace of their midnight bathes. Not a single article of clothing left behind on the Polynesian totem pole.

"If you'd like to stay here for a few days, you can," he said. "You won't be in our way."

I was tempted to say yes. Once again that tenderness, that feeling of exaltation swept over me, as it had when I was walking down the sloping street with her. To allow oneself to live from day to day. To stop asking oneself questions about the future. To be in the company of kindly people who help you to get over your difficulties, and give you gradual confidence in yourself.

"I have to go back to Paris ... For my work ..."

They offered to drive me to the station in Saint-Raphaël. No, it was no trouble. In any case, they had to visit the Les Issandres house again. This time he drove, and I got into the back.

"I hope you won't be frightened," she said, turning towards me. "He drives even worse than we do."

He drove too fast, and I often had to cling on to the seat at the bends. My hand finally strayed on to her shoulder, and just as I was about to take it away he braked violently because of another bend, which made her grip my wrist very hard.

"He's going to kill us," she said.

"No, no, don't worry. It won't be for this time."

At the station in Saint-Raphaël he made his way rapidly to the booking office, while she kept me back at the bookstall.

"Could you find me a detective story?" she asked.

I looked through the shelves and chose a book in the *Série Noire*.

"That'll do," she said.

He joined us. He handed me a ticket.

"I got you a first class one. It'll be more comfortable."

27

I was embarrassed. I tried to find the words to thank him. "You didn't need..."

He shrugged his shoulders and bought a book in the *Série Noire*. Then they came with me on to the platform. There were about ten minutes to wait for the train. We all three sat down on a bench.

"I'd very much like to see you again," I said.

"We have a phone number in Paris. We shall probably be there this winter."

He took a pen out of the inner pocket of his jacket, tore the endpaper out of his detective novel and wrote his name and phone number on it. Then he folded the page and gave it to me.

I got into the carriage, and they both stood by the door, waiting for the train to start.

"You'll be left in peace..." he said. "There's no one in these compartments."

As the train began to move, she took off her sunglasses and I met her pale blue or grey eyes again.

"Good luck," she said.

At Marseilles, I went through my travel bag to make sure I had my passport, and I discovered, tucked under the collar of a shirt, a few bank notes. I wondered whether it was she or he who had had the idea of leaving me this money. Perhaps both at the same time.

I took advantage of the fourteenth of July to creep into our flat in the Cité Véron without attracting anyone's attention. I went up the staircase that no one uses any more, behind the Moulin Rouge. On the third floor, the door opens on to a utility room. Before my false departure for Rio de Janeiro I had taken the key to this door – an old Bricard key whose existence Annette has no suspicion of – and conspicuously left on my bedside table the only key she knows, the one to the front door of the flat. So even if she had guessed that I'd stayed in Paris, she knew that I had left my key behind, and consequently that it was impossible for me to get into the flat unexpectedly.

No light in the utility room. I groped my way to the handle of the door that opens on to a little bedroom, which would have been called "the children's room" if Annette and I had had any. A booklined corridor leads to the big room we use as a salon. I walked on tiptoe, but I was in no danger. They were all up above, on the terrace. I could hear the murmur of their conversation. Life was continuing without me. For a moment I was tempted to climb the narrow stairs with their plaited-rope hand rail and their life buoys hanging on the walls. I should come out on to the terrace which resembles the upper deck of a liner, because Annette and I had wanted our flat to give us the impression of always being on a cruise:

portholes, gangways, rails . . . I should come out on to the terrace, and what I might describe as a deathly silence would fall. Then, when they'd got over their surprise, they'd ask me questions, they'd make a fuss of me, there would be even greater gaiety than usual and they'd drink champagne in honour of the revenant.

But I stopped on the first step. No, decidedly, I had no wish to see anyone, or to talk, or to give any explanations, or to carry on with my old life as before. I wanted to go into our bedroom to get a few summer clothes and a pair of moccasins. I turned the doorhandle gently. It was locked on the inside. Below, on the carpet, a thin shaft of light. A couple had left the party while it was in full swing. Who? Annette and Cavanaugh? My widow – for wasn't she my widow if I decided never to reappear? – was she occupying the conjugal bed at this moment with my best friend?

I went into the adjoining room, which I use as a study. The communicating door was ajar. I recognized Annette's voice.

"No, no . . . My darling . . . Don't be afraid . . . No one's going to come and disturb us . . ."

"Are you sure? Anyone could leave the terrace and come in here . . . Especially Cavanaugh . . ."

"No, no . . . Cavanaugh won't come . . . I locked the door . . ."

From the gentle, protective tones of Annette's first words, I could tell that she wasn't with Cavanaugh. Then I recognized the muffled voice of Ben Smidane, a young man we had elected to the Explorers' Club at the beginning of the year, with Cavanaugh and me as sponsors, a young man who wanted to dedicate himself to searching for the wrecks of boats that had gone down in the Indian Ocean and the Pacific, and who Annette had said had "the face of a Greek shepherd".

*

30

The light went out in the bedroom, and Annette said in a hoarse voice:

"Don't be afraid, my darling..."

Then I shut the door gently and switched on the light in my study. I searched the drawers until I found an old dark-green cardboard folder. I put it under my arm and left the room, abandoning my widow and Ben Smidane to their amours.

I stood still for a moment in the middle of the corridor, listening to the hum of the conversation. I thought of Cavanaugh up there, a glass of champagne in his hand, standing at the ship's rail. With the other guests he would be gazing at the Place Blanche which looked like a little fishing port they were about to put into. Unless he had noticed Annette's prolonged absence and was wondering where on earth my widow could have got to.

I saw myself again, twenty years earlier, with Ingrid and Rigaud, in the semi-darkness outside the bungalow. Around us, shouts and bursts of laughter similar to those now reaching me from the terrace. I was now about the same age as Ingrid and Rigaud were then, and whereas their attitude had seemed to me so strange then, I shared it this evening. I remembered what Ingrid had said: "We'll pretend to be dead."

I went down the secret stairway, behind the Moulin Rouge, and found myself back on the boulevard. I crossed the Place Blanche and raised my head in the direction of our terrace. Up there, there was no danger of them spotting me among the crowds of tourists being disgorged from the coaches, and the people out for a stroll on the fourteenth of July. Did they still spare just a little thought for me? Deep down I was very fond of them: my widow, Cavanaugh, Ben Smidane and the other guests. One day I'll come back to you. I don't yet know the precise date of my resurrection. I shall have to have the strength and the inclination. But this evening I'm going to take the métro to the Porte Dorée. Light. So detached from everything.

When I got back, around midnight, the fountains in the square were still illuminated and a few groups, among which I noticed some children, were making their way towards the entrance to the zoo. It had stayed open for the fourteenth of July, and no doubt the animals would remain in their cages and enclosures, half asleep. Why shouldn't I too pay them a nocturnal visit, and thus have the illusion of making our old dream come true: letting ourselves be locked in the zoo overnight?

But I preferred to go back to the Dodds Hotel and lie down on the little cherry-wood bed in my room. I reread the pages contained in the dark-green folder. Notes, and even short chapters, that I'd written ten years ago, the rough draft of a project cherished at the time: to write Ingrid's biography.

It was September, in Paris, and for the first time I had begun to have doubts about my life and profession. From then on I would have to share Annette, my wife, with Cavanaugh, my best friend. The public had lost interest in the documentaries we were bringing back from the antipodes. All those journeys, those countries where they had monsoons, earthquakes, amoebas and virgin forests, had lost their charm for me. Had they ever had any?

Days of doubt and depression. I had five weeks' respite before dragging myself across Asia on the route followed by the 1931 car expedition across central Asia. I cursed the members of that expedition, whose tyre tracks I was obliged to discover. Never had Paris, the *quais* along the Seine, and the Place Blanche seemed so attractive. How stupid to leave all that once again . . .

The memory of Ingrid was obsessing me, and I had spent the days before my departure in noting down everything I knew about her, which is to say not much . . . After the war, Rigaud and Ingrid had lived in the Midi for five or six years, but I had no information about that period. Then Ingrid had gone to America, without Rigaud. She had gone with a film producer. This producer had wanted her to be an extra in a few unimportant films. Rigaud had joined her, she had abandoned the producer and the cinema. She had again separated from Rigaud, who went back to France, and she had spent more years in America – years about which I knew nothing. Then she had returned to France, and Paris. And some time later, to Rigaud. And we were coming to the time when I had met them on the Saint-Raphaël road.

I found it distasteful to read all my notes ten years later; it was as if someone else had written them. For instance, the chapter entitled "The American Years". Was I definitely sure that they had loomed so large in her existence?

With time, this episode took on a trivial and almost ridiculous aspect. But when I wrote these notes I was more susceptible to irrelevances and glitter, and I didn't go straight to the nub. How childish it was of me to have cut out from a 1951 magazine a colour photo of the Champs-Élysées at night, in summer, under the pretext that it was in the summer of 1951, on one of the terraces in the Avenue, that Ingrid had made the acquaintance of the American producer . . . I had attached this document to my notes, to give a better feeling of the atmosphere in which Ingrid lived when she was twenty-five. The sun umbrellas and the cane chairs on the terraces, the look of a seaside resort that the Avenue des Champs-Élysées still had then, the softness of the Paris evenings that suited her youth so well ... And the name I had noted: Alexandre d'Arc, an old Frenchman from Hollywood, the man who, that evening, had introduced Ingrid to the producer, because he accompanied him on all his trips to Europe and was given the job of seeing that he met what in those days they called young persons ...

Among my notes was another document that I'd thought necessary to Ingrid's biography: a photo of the American producer, discovered by chance during my researches. This photo had been taken during a gala evening in a Florida casino. Some gymnasts were performing on a stage in the middle of the room, and all of a sudden the producer, wanting to impress Ingrid, had got up from the table and taken off his dinner jacket, bow tie and shirt. Stripped to the waist, he had climbed up on to the stage and, in front of the flabbergasted gymnasts, grabbed hold of the trapeze. The photo showed him hanging from the trapeze, his chest thrust out, his stomach held in, his legs at right angles. He was very short, and he wore a moustache that followed the line of his lip, which reminded me of distant childhood memories. His jaws clenched, his chest triumphant, his legs at right angles ...

This man was trying to prove to a woman who could have been his daughter that you can possess eternal youth. When she told me this anecdote, Ingrid laughed just as hard as I did, until the tears came into her eyes. I wonder whether those tears were not due to the thought of all the time she had wasted in futile evenings like that one.

I tore the photograph of the Avenue des Champs-Élysées and the one of the producer into tiny pieces, which I jumbled up and then scattered in the wastepaper basket. The page on Alexandre d'Arc suffered the same fate; ten years ago his phoney name and the fact that he was a pimp by profession had struck me as so romantic that I had considered the fellow worthy of figuring in a biography of Ingrid. I felt a vague twinge of remorse: has a biographer the right to suppress certain details under the pretext that he considers them superfluous? Or do they all have their importance, and must he present them one after the other, impartially, so that not a single one is left out, as in the inventory of a distraint?

Unless the line of a life, once it has reached its term, purges itself of all its useless and decorative elements. In which case, all that remains is the essential: the blanks, the silences and the pauses. I finally fell asleep, turning all these serious questions over in my mind.

*

The next morning, in the café on the corner of the square and the Boulevard Soult, a girl and boy who weren't much over twenty were sitting at the table next to mine, and they smiled at me. I felt an urge to talk to them. I thought them well suited to each other; he was dark and she was fair. Perhaps that was how Annette and I had looked at the same age. I found their presence reassuring, and they communicated something of their mysterious power and freshness to me, because I was in good spirits for the rest of the day.

That boy and girl made me reflect on my first meeting with Ingrid and Rigaud on the Saint-Raphaël road. I wondered why they'd stopped their car and invited me to their place so very naturally. It was as if they'd always known me. I'd spent a sleepless night in the train, of course, and my fatigue gave me the impression that everything was possible and that life had lost all its rough edges: all you had to do was let yourself slide down a gentle slope, raise your arm, and a car would stop and people would help you without even asking you any questions. You fell asleep under the pine trees, and when you woke up two pale blue eyes were gazing at you. When I walked down the Rue de la Citadelle arm in arm with Ingrid, it was with the certainty that for the first time in my life I was under someone's protection.

But I hadn't forgotten the way Rigaud limped, as slightly as possible, as if he was trying to hide an injury, or the words Ingrid had whispered in the dark: We'll pretend to be dead. They must already have felt, both of them, that they were coming to the end of the road. At least Ingrid must have. Perhaps my presence had been a distraction for them and a passing comfort. Perhaps, fleetingly, I had conjured up a memory of youth for them. For in fact it was at my age that they had found themselves on the Côte d'Azur. They were very much on their own. And orphans. That must have been why Ingrid had wanted to know whether I had parents.

I didn't need to consult my notes that evening in my room in the Dodds Hotel. I remembered everything as if it had been yesterday ... They had arrived on the Côte d'Azur in the spring of 1942. She was sixteen, and he was twenty-one. They didn't get off the train at Saint-Raphaël, as I had done, but at Juan-les-Pins. They had come from Paris, and had crossed the demarcation line illegally. Ingrid had a false identity card in the name of Ingrid Teyrsen, married name Rigaud, which aged her by three years. Rigaud had hidden several hundreds of thousands of francs in the linings of his jackets and at the bottom of his suit-case.

They were the only passengers at Juan-les-Pins that morning. A cab was waiting outside the station, a black cab with a white horse. They decided to take it, because of their suitcases. The horse started off at a walk, and they crossed the deserted square in the pine forest. The cabdriver's head was leaning over to the right. From behind, it looked as if he had fallen asleep. At the bend in the road leading to the Cape, the sea appeared. The cab turned into a steep alleyway. The driver cracked his whip, and the horse broke into a trot. Then it jerked to a halt outside the enormous white mass of the Hôtel Provençal.

"We must tell them we're on honeymoon," Rigaud had said.

*

Only one floor of the hotel was still in use, and the rare guests seemed to be living there in hiding. Before reaching it, the lift slowly passed whole floors of shadow and silence, where it would never stop again. Anyone who wanted to use the stairs needed a torch. The big dining room was closed, its chandelier enveloped in a white sheet. The bar wasn't in use, either. So the guests gathered in a corner of the lobby.

Their room was at the back of the hotel and looked out on to a road that sloped gently down to the beach. Their balcony overlooked the pine forest, and they often saw the cab going round the bend in the road to the Cape. In the evenings, the silence was so deep that the clicking sound of the horse's hooves took a very long time to die away. Ingrid and Rigaud played a game to see which of them had such sharp ears as to be the last to hear the horse's hooves.

*

At Juan-les-Pins, people behaved as if the war didn't exist. The men wore beach trousers and the women light-coloured pareus. All these people were some twenty years older than Ingrid and Rigaud, but this was barely noticeable. Owing to their suntanned skin and their athletic gait, they still looked young and falsely carefree. They didn't know the way things would go when the summer was over. At aperitif time, they exchanged addresses. Would they be able to get rooms in Megève this winter? Some preferred the Val-d'Isère, and were already getting ready to book accommodation at the Col de l'Iseran. Others had no intention of leaving the Côte d'Azur. It was possible that they were going to reopen the Altitude 43 in Saint-Tropez, that white hotel which looks like a liner grounded among the pines above the Plage de la Bouillabaisse. They would be safe there. Fleeting signs of anguish could be read on their faces under the suntan: to think that they were going to have to be permanently on the move, searching for a place that the war had spared, and that these oases were going to become rarer all the time ... Rationing was beginning on the Côte. You mustn't think about anything, so as not to undermine your morale. These idle days sometimes gave you the feeling of being under house arrest. You had to create a vacuum in your head. Let yourself be gently numbed by the sun and the swaying of the palm trees in the breeze ... Shut your eyes. Ingrid and Rigaud lived the same sort of life as these people who were forgetting the war, but they kept out of their way and avoided speaking to them. At first, everyone had been astonished by their youth. Were they waiting for their parents? Were they on holiday? Rigaud had replied that Ingrid and he "were on honeymoon", quite simply. And this reply, far from surprising them, had reassured the guests at the Provençal. If young people still went on honeymoon, it meant that the situation wasn't so tragic as all that and that the earth was still going round.

In the mornings they went down to the beach which stretched below the pine forest between the Casino and the beginning of the road to the Cape. The hotel's private beach, with its pergola and its bathing huts wasn't functioning now "as it did in peacetime", as the hall porter put it. A few deck chairs and sunshades were still at the guests' disposal. But they weren't allowed to use the bathing huts until the end of the war. Newcomers wondered whether they weren't committing an offence when they used this beach. They were even a little ashamed of sunbathing. In the first days, Rigaud had to reassure Ingrid, who was always afraid that someone would come and ask them what they were doing there, because she was still suffering from the after-effects of the precarious life she had lived in Paris. He had bought her a pale green swimming costume in a boutique in Juan-les-Pins. And also a pareu, with pastel-coloured printed designs, like the other women wore. They would lie on a pontoon, and as soon as the sun had dried their skin they dived into the sea again. They would swim out, and then return to the beach side by side, swimming on their backs. At the beginning of the afternoon, when the sun was too hot, they would cross the deserted road and walk up the path lined with pines and palm trees that led to the entrance to the Provençal. Often, the hall porter was not at the reception desk. But Rigaud kept their key in his bath-robe pocket. Then there would be the slow ascent in the lift, the dark landings going by, leaving them to imagine the silent, interminable corridors, the rooms which probably contained no more than their bed-frames. As the lift rose, the air became lighter, and they were enveloped in the coolness of the half light. On the fifth floor, the big wrought-iron gate would bang behind them, and then nothing else would break the silence.

From their balcony they gazed down at the pine forest, and under its dark-green fringe they could make out the white patch of the casino. And along the wall round the hotel, the steep street where nobody went by. Then they closed their shutters – pale-green shutters, the same colour as Ingrid's swimming costume.

*

In the evenings, they would cross the square in the pine forest and go and have dinner at the only restaurant in Juan-les-Pins that ignored the restrictions. Customers came there from Nice and Cannes. At the beginning, Ingrid felt ill at ease there.

The habitués greeted each other from table to table, the men tied their sweaters casually over their shoulders, the women showed their tanned backs and swathed their hair in creole foulards. You could overhear conversations in English. The war was so far away ... The restaurant was in a wing of a building near the casino and its tables spilled over on to the pavement. It was said that the *patronne* – a certain Mademoiselle Cotillon – had had a brush with the law, but that these days she enjoyed "protection". She was very pleasant, and in Juan-les-Pins she was known as the Princesse de Bourbon.

*

They went back to the hotel, and on moonless nights a feeling of anxiety descended on them both. Not a single street lamp, not a single lighted window. The Princess de Bourbon's restaurant was still aglow, as if she was the last to dare to defy the curfew. But after a few steps this light disappeared, and they were walking in the dark. The murmur of conversation faded, too. All those people whose presence at the tables reassured them, and whom they saw on the beach during the day, now seemed unreal: walkers-on from a touring company who had got stuck in Juan-les-Pins because of the war and were compelled to play their parts of phoney holidaymakers on the beach and in the restaurant run by a phoney Princesse de Bourbon. The Provençal itself, whose white mass could just be made out in the shadows in the background, was a gigantic pasteboard set.

And every time they crossed this dark pine forest, Ingrid was suddenly shaken by sobs.

*

But they went into the lobby. The glittering light of the chandelier made them blink. The porter was standing behind the reception desk in his uniform. He smiled, and gave them the key to their room. Things regained a little consistence and reality. They found themselves in a real hotel lobby with real walls and a real uniformed porter. Then they went up in the lift. And once again they became a prey to doubt and anxiety when they pressed the button for the fifth floor, as all the buttons for the other floors were covered with sticky tape to make it quite clear that they were not in use.

At the end of their long ascent in the dark, they came to a landing and a corridor faintly lit by naked bulbs. That was the way it was. They went from light to shade and from shade to light. They had to get used to this world in which everything could fluctuate from one moment to the next.

*

In the mornings, when they opened the shutters, a harsh light flooded into the room. It was exactly like the summers of the past. The dark green of the pines, the blue sky, the scent of eucalyptus and oleanders from the Avenue Saramartel which goes down to the beach . . . In the heat haze, the Provençal's great white façade soared upwards for all eternity and you had the impression that this monument protected you, if you gazed at it from the pontoon, lying there after your swim.

Just one very small detail was enough to blot this landscape: a dark patch Rigaud had noticed for the first time, late one afternoon, on a bench in one of the paths in the pine forest. Ingrid and he were coming back from a walk on the boulevard along the coast. A man in a city suit was sitting on the bench, reading a newspaper. And in contrast to the dark colour of his suit, his complexion was milky white, like that of someone who never exposes himself to the sun.

The next morning they were both lying on the pontoon. And Rigaud again noticed this dark patch leaning on the balustrade of the terrace, to the left of the steps leading down to the beach. The man was watching the few people who were sunbathing. Rigaud was the only one who saw him, as the others had their backs to him. For a moment he had wanted to point him out to Ingrid, but he changed his mind. He got her into the sea, they swam even farther out than usual, and then returned to the pontoon, swimming on their backs. Ingrid preferred to stay on the beach, as the pontoon was scorching. Rigaud had gone to fetch her a deck chair from the veranda outside the bathing huts. He went back to Ingrid, who was standing at the edge of the water in her pale-green swimming costume, and looked up towards the balustrade. This time the man seemed to be spying on Ingrid, smoking a cigarette which remained glued to his lips. His face was still as milk white, in spite of the sun. And his suit appeared even darker in contrast with the white veranda and beach huts. Rigaud had spotted him once again at aperitif time, sitting at the far end of the lobby, staring at the guests coming out of the lift.

*

So far, he hadn't been able to see his features very clearly. But that same evening, in the Princesse de Bourbon's restaurant, he was able to do so at leisure. The man was sitting at a table near theirs, at the back of the room. A bony face. Blond hair with reddish glints, combed back. His milk-white skin seemed to be pitted over his cheekbones. He was wearing his city suit and casting a beady eye over the tables where the habitués were sitting. It was almost as if he wanted to take a census of them. Finally his gaze came to rest on Ingrid and Rigaud.

"Are you on holiday?"

He had tried to soften the metallic tone of his voice as if attempting to worm a shameful secret out of them. Ingrid turned her head towards him.

"Not exactly," Rigaud said. "We're on honeymoon."

"On honeymoon?"

With a nod, he expressed feigned admiration. Then he took a cigarette holder out of his jacket pocket, stuck a Caporal in it – the packet was on the table – lit it and took a long puff, which hollowed his cheeks.

"You're lucky to be on honeymoon."

"Lucky? Do you really think so?"

Rigaud regretted the insolent manner in which he had replied. He had stared at the man with wide-open eyes, pretending to be astonished.

"Given the circumstances, very few people your age can indulge in a honeymoon . . ."

Once again that smooth tone. Ingrid remained silent. Rigaud guessed that she was embarrassed and would have liked to leave the restaurant.

"Can you stand those cigarettes?" Rigaud asked the man, pointing to the packet of Caporal on the table.

A sudden impulse. It was too late to go back on it now. The man was looking at him, screwing up his eyes. Rigaud heard himself say:

"Don't they make your throat sore? I have some English ones, if you like."

And he held out a packet of Craven A.

"I don't smoke English cigarettes," said the man, with a twisted smile. "I can't afford them."

Then he began to study the menu, and thereafter pretended to ignore Ingrid and Rigaud. He went on indefatigably looking from table to table, as if he wanted to engrave everyone's face in his memory and take notes later on.

*

When they were back at the hotel, Rigaud regretted his childishly provocative gesture. He had found the packet of Craven A, empty, in the drawer of the bedside table, left there by a guest from the palmy prewar days. Ingrid and he were leaning over the balcony. Below, the roof of the church and the umbrella pines were silhouetted in the moonlight. The terrace of the Princesse de Bourbon's restaurant was hidden under the foliage.

45

"Who can that fellow be?" Ingrid asked.

"I don't know."

If he had been on his own, he wouldn't have been at all worried by the presence of that man. Since the beginning of the war he had never been afraid of anything, but he was afraid for Ingrid.

*

Often, the dark patch – as Rigaud called him – remained invisible. They might almost have thought that the sun in Juan-les-Pins had caused it to vanish for ever. Unfortunately, it reappeared in places where they no longer expected it. On the balustrade of the beach when people were bathing. On the pavement of the road to the Cape. On the terrace of the casino. One evening, when Rigaud was just about to take the lift up to join Ingrid in their room, he heard a metallic voice behind him:

"Still on honeymoon?"

He turned round. The man was in front of him, looking fondly at him.

"Yes. Still on honeymoon."

He had replied in the most neutral way possible. Because of Ingrid.

*

One night he woke up at about three o'clock, and opened the window because of the stifling heat. Ingrid was asleep, and she had folded the sheet down at the foot of the bed. A glint of moonlight lit up her shoulder and the curve of her hip. He felt nervous, and couldn't get back to sleep. He got up, and tiptoed out of the room to see if he could get a packet of cigarettes. The light from the bulbs in the corridor was even dimmer than usual. The one in the lift was out, but downstairs the chandelier was shining very brightly.

He was just about to cross the lobby when he saw the dark patch behind the reception desk. The man was alone, bending over a wide-open register and taking notes. He hadn't seen Rigaud, and there was still time for him to turn round and go back up to his room. But like the other evening, at the Princesse de Bourbon's restaurant, a sudden impulse came over him. He walked slowly over to the reception desk. The man was still absorbed in his work. When he got up to him, Rigaud put both his hands down flat on the marble. Then the man raised his head, and produced a stony smile.

"I've come to get a packet of cigarettes," said Rigaud.

"Craven A, I suppose?"

It was the same smooth tone as the other evening.

"But I'm disturbing you in your work. I'll come back later."

And Rigaud openly bent over the book in which the man was writing his notes: a list of names that he had copied, the names of the guests written in the hotel register. The man snapped his notebook shut.

"As there aren't any Craven A, maybe you'd like one of these? . . ."

He offered him his packet of Caporal.

"No, thank you."

Rigaud had said that in a pleasant tone. He didn't take his eyes off the big hotel register, open in front of him.

"Were you taking notes?"

"I was gathering some information. And while I work, *you* are on honeymoon . . ."

As he had the other evening, he gave Rigaud a fond look. And his smile revealed a gold tooth.

Rigaud had lowered his head. In front of him, the dark patch of the suit. A crumpled suit. A too-small black tie hung down from the collar of the brown shirt. The man had lit a cigarette. Ash fell on to the lapels of his jacket. Rigaud suddenly noticed a strange smell – a mixture of tobacco, sweat, and violet scent.

"I'm really sorry to be on honeymoon," said Rigaud. "But that's the way it is ... And it can't be any other way ..."

Then he turned his back and crossed the lobby to the lift. When he reached the gate, he gazed at the man over at the reception desk. The other was also staring at him. And under Rigaud's insistent look, he finally went back to his work, trying to make it look as natural as possible. He leafed through the hotel register, and from time to time wrote something in his notebook – no doubt the name of a guest, which had escaped his attention.

*

In the room, Ingrid was still asleep. Rigaud sat down at the foot of the bed and looked at her smooth, childish face. He knew he wouldn't be able to go back to sleep.

He went and leaned against the balcony. He could still watch over her from there. Ingrid's left cheek was resting on her outstretched arm. Her hand was floating in space. He heard the click of hooves that heralded the passage of the cab and wondered whether he wasn't imagining things. Why that cab, so late? The sound came nearer and he leaned over the balcony, hoping to see the white horse go by. But a clump of pines concealed the bend in the Cape road.

The sound of the hooves grew fainter, and he couldn't play with Ingrid at seeing which of them would be the last to hear it. He shut his eyes. The sound was now almost imperceptible, down there on the road. It would fade completely, and then nothing would break the silence. He imagined himself sitting beside Ingrid in the cab going along the road. He leaned over to the driver and asked him the purpose of the journey, but the cabbie had fallen asleep. So had Ingrid. Her head had dropped down on to his shoulder, and he felt her breath in the hollow of his neck. Now he and the white horse were the only ones still awake. In his case, it was anguish that prevented him from sleeping. But the white horse? What if it suddenly stopped in the middle of the road, in the dead of night?

*

The next morning they were sunbathing on the pontoon, and from time to time Rigaud raised his head up to the balustrade overlooking the beach to check whether the dark patch was there. No, though. It had vanished. For how long? At what moment, at what spot in Juan-les-Pins would it reappear?

Ingrid had left her big beach hat in their room.

"I'll go and fetch it."

"Oh no. Stay here."

"Yes. I'll go."

It was an excuse to leave the beach for a moment without alarming Ingrid. He wanted to check whether the man was in the vicinity. He would feel more relaxed if he knew where he was. But he was neither in the hotel gardens nor in the lobby. Beach hat in hand, Rigaud detoured through the Rue de l'Oratoire which led to the pine forest. The sun was oppressive, and he kept to the shady pavement. Walking some ten metres in front of him was a very tall, slightly stooping man. He recognized the hotel porter.

The beach hat was like one his mother had worn years before. Ingrid had bought it in a boutique near the casino, where it had been the only hat in the window. Someone – perhaps his mother – had left it behind in Juan-les-Pins at the end of one summer, like the empty packet of Craven A he had found in the back of the drawer.

The porter was walking slowly in front of him, and he didn't want to pass him. He remembered the villa, on the Cape road, where his mother sometimes used to take him to visit an American woman friend. On those days they left Cannes after lunch. He was between ten and twelve. The visit to the American friend lasted until the evening. There were a lot of

49

people in the salon and on the landing stage down below. All of them were interested in water skiing, and the American had been the first woman to take it up. He remembered one of the guests very clearly: a suntanned man with white hair whose body was as dry as that of a mummy, and who was also very keen on water skiing. Each time, his mother would point out this guest and say: "Go and say hallo to Monsieur Bailby", before abandoning him in the garden where he played by himself all afternoon. Unpleasant memories. They had come back to him because of the hall porter now walking in front of him. He caught him up, and put a hand on his shoulder. The man turned round, surprised, and smiled at him:

"You're a guest at the hotel, if I'm not mistaken?"

Rigaud felt impulsively drawn towards this man. He had been in such distress since the day before, he was so very frightened that something dreadful could happen to Ingrid, that he was ready to cling to any life buoy.

"I'm Madame Paul Rigaud's son . . ."

The words had escaped him, and he felt like laughing. Why suddenly bring up his mother, a woman who had so little maternal feeling that she abandoned him for whole days in the garden of the villa, and one evening had even forgotten he was there and left without him? Some time later, when he was dying of hunger and cold in a boarding school in the Alps, the only thing she had seen fit to send him was a silk shirt.

"Are you really Madame Paul Rigaud's son?"

The man was looking at him as if he were the Prince of Wales.

"But you ought to have told me before, Monsieur, that you were her son . . ."

The porter had straightened his back and seemed so moved that Rigaud felt he had pronounced a magic formula. He wondered whether he hadn't chosen Juan-les-Pins for a refuge because it was linked to his childhood. A sad, but sheltered childhood, in a world that still believed it would last for ever, or that was too frivolous to think of the future. For instance, his mother, that poor feather-brained creature . . . She would really not have understood the first thing about the war, or about the ghost-like Juan-les-Pins of today, where people lived from the black market with false papers in their pockets. But here he was, using her as a last resort.

"I remember Madame Paul Rigaud so well . . . She used to come to meet her friends here, in Juan . . . And you – you're her son . . ."

He gave him a protective look. Rigaud felt sure that this man could help him.

"I'd like to ask your advice," he stammered. "I'm in a delicate situation . . ."

"We'll be able to talk better here."

He led him under the archway of a big white building whose roofs and deserted playground Rigaud could see from their balcony: L'École Saint-Philippe. They emerged on to one of the playgrounds with a covered passageway at the far end, and the porter guided him to a plane tree at the side of the ground. He pointed to a bench at the foot of the plane tree:

"Sit down."

He sat down beside Rigaud.

"I'm listening."

This man could have been his grandfather, and had white hair and long legs, which he crossed. And he looked like an Englishman or an American.

"It's like this . . .," Rigaud began, in a hesitant voice. "I came here from Paris with a girl . . ."

"Your wife, if I'm not mistaken?"

"She isn't my wife . . . I got her some false papers . . . She had to leave Paris . . ."

"I understand . . ."

And what if it was all only a bad dream? How could the

war have any semblance of reality when you found yourself sitting under a plane tree in a playground, in the provincial calm of an early afternoon? At the other end, the classrooms, and beside you a man with white hair and an affectionate voice who had tender memories of your mother. And the reassuring, monotonous chirping of the crickets.

"You can't stay at the hotel any longer," said the porter. "But I'll find you another refuge . . ."

"Do you really think we can't stay?" Rigaud murmured.

"Next week the police are going to raid all the hotels on the Côte."

A cat sidled out of the half-open door of one of the class-rooms, crossed the covered passageway and went and curled up in the middle of a pool of sunlight. And they could still hear the crickets chirping.

"We've already been inspected by a man sent specially from Paris."

"I know," said Rigaud. "A man in a dark suit. Do you think he's still here?"

"Unfortunately, yes," said the porter. "He circulates between Cannes and Nice. He insists on checking all the hotel registers."

Rigaud had put Ingrid's beach hat down on the bench beside him. She would be getting worried because he hadn't come back. He would have liked her to be with them in this play-ground, where you felt safe. Over there, the cat was asleep in the middle of the pool of sunlight.

"Do you think we could hide here?" Rigaud asked.

And he pointed to the classrooms and to the first floor, where the dormitories must be.

"I have a better hiding place for you," said the porter. "The villa of an American lady your mother used to see a lot of in the old days."

*

52

On his way to the beach, Rigaud considered what he was going to say to Ingrid. He wouldn't tell her that police raids were expected the following week, but simply say that a friend of his mother was lending them her villa. His mother ... Through what irony of fate was she now so persistently reappearing in his life, whereas before, she had never been there when he needed her? And now that she was dead, it was as if Madame Paul Rigaud wanted to be forgiven and to obliterate all the wrong she had done him.

The beach was deserted. The few deck chairs still facing the sea hadn't even been folded. No one was there but Ingrid. She was sunbathing on the pontoon.

"I met the porter from the Provençal," Rigaud said. "He's found us a villa. The hotel's going to close soon."

Ingrid had sat down on the edge of the pontoon, her legs dangling. She had put on the big hat, which concealed her face.

"It's odd," she said. "They all left at the same time."

Rigaud couldn't take his eyes off the empty deck chairs.

"They must have gone to have a siesta ..."

But he knew very well that on the other days, at the same time, there had still been people on the beach.

"Shall we bathe?" said Ingrid.

"Yes."

She had taken off her hat and put it on the pontoon. They dived. The sea was as calm as a lake. They swam breast stroke, about fifty metres. Rigaud raised his head slightly in the direction of the beach and the pontoon. Ingrid's big hat formed a red patch on the dark wood. That was the only sign of any human presence in the vicinity.

*

They left the beach at around five, and Rigaud wanted to buy a newspaper. Ingrid was amazed. Ever since they had been in

Juan-les-Pins they hadn't read a single paper, except a film magazine that Ingrid bought each week.

But the newsagent was closed. And all the shops in the Rue Guy-de-Maupassant had already lowered their blinds. They were the only people walking along the pavement. They turned back.

"Don't you think it's strange?" Ingrid asked.

"No ... Not at all ..." said Rigaud, forcing himself to speak casually. "The season's over ... And we didn't realize it ..."

"Why did you want to buy a paper? Has something happened?"

"No."

The square in the pine forest was also deserted. And on the strip of ground where games of bowls were usually going on, not a single player: had the inhabitants of Juan-les-Pins also left their town, like the holiday-makers?

Outside the entrance to the Provençal, the cab with the white horse was waiting, and the driver was just finishing loading it with a pile of suitcases. Then he climbed up on to his seat and cracked his whip. The horse, walking even more slowly than usual, started off down the hotel drive. Ingrid and Rigaud stood at the door for a moment, waiting to hear the sound of the hooves grow fainter.

Rigaud was filled with apprehension, which Ingrid must have shared, as she said:

"Maybe there's going to be an earthquake ..."

And the sunlight all around them deepened the silence.

*

In the hotel lobby – no one. At this time of day the guests were usually sitting at the tables at the far end, having their aperitifs, and when Ingrid and Rigaud came back from the beach they were greeted by the murmur of conversation.

The hall porter was standing behind the reception desk.

"You can spend one more night here. Tomorrow, I'll take you to the villa."

"Are we the only ones left?" Rigaud asked.

"Yes. The others left after lunch. Because of an article yesterday in a Paris paper . . ."

He turned to the pigeonholes behind him, where a few now useless keys were hanging.

"I've changed your room," said the porter. "It's wiser . . . You're on the first floor . . . I'll bring you up some dinner later . . ."

"Have you got the article?" Rigaud asked.

"Yes."

This time they went up the stairs and along the corridor lit by a nightlight, to Room 116. The blinds were drawn, but even so the sun filtered through and formed little rectangles of light on the floor. There was just a bare bed-frame. Rigaud went over to one of the windows and unfolded the paper the porter had given him. The headline of the article, on the front page, hit him in the eye: "The Perfumed Ghetto . . . Who's Who in the hotels on the Côte d'Azur." A list of names at the start of the article. His name wasn't there, as it sounded French.

"What does the article say?" Ingrid asked.

"Nothing of any interest . . ."

He folded the paper and stuffed it into the drawer of the bedside table. A few years hence, when the war was over and the hotel was once again full of life, a guest would discover this paper as he, Rigaud, had found the empty packet of Craven A. He went and lay down beside Ingrid on the bed-frame and held her close to him. There was not even any point now in picking up the card on the bedside table and hanging it outside the door: "Do not disturb."

*

55

He slept fitfully. He woke up suddenly and made sure that Ingrid was still lying beside him on the frame. He had wanted to lock the door, but that was a useless precaution: the porter had given him a master key which opened the communicating doors between the rooms.

Some men guided by the dark patch had entered the lobby and were about to raid the hotel. But he wasn't at all afraid for Ingrid. The men were going along the corridors on all five floors with torches which barely pierced the darkness. And they'd have to open, one after the other, the doors to the two hundred and fifty rooms in the hotel to check whether or not they were occupied.

He could hear the regular banging of the doors on the upper floors. The bangs came nearer, and occasionally he heard voices: the dark patch and the others had now reached their floor. His hand tightened on the master key. As soon as he heard them open the door to the room next to theirs he would wake Ingrid and they'd slip into the room on the other side. And this game of cat and mouse would continue through all the rooms on the floor. The men really hadn't the slightest chance of finding them, because they'd both be hidden in the depths of the shadows of the Provençal.

Once again he awoke with a start. Not a sound. Not the slightest banging of a door. The blinds let the daylight through. He turned to Ingrid. Her cheek resting on her arm, she was sleeping like the child she was.

*

At the end of the palm-lined drive stood the villa, with its medieval-style façade surmounted by a turret. At the time when he used to come here with his mother, Rigaud was reading Walter Scott, and he imagined that the castles in *Ivan-hoe* or *Quentin Durward* were like this villa. The first time he came, he had been surprised that the American woman and

"Monsieur Bailby" were not dressed like the people in the illustrations of these books.

The porter wanted to show them the garden first.

"I know it by heart," Rigaud said.

He could have walked down the paths with his eyes shut. Over there were the well and the phoney Roman ruins, and the big lawn cut like an English one which made a contrast with the umbrella pines and oleanders. And over there, at the edge of the lawn, was where he'd been when his mother had forgotten all about him one evening and gone back to Cannes without him.

"You'll be safe here."

The porter looked round the garden. Rigaud tried to conquer his uneasy feeling by gripping Ingrid's arm. He had the unpleasant impression that he was returning to his point of departure, to the scene of his unhappy childhood, and that he was sensing the invisible presence of his mother, just when he had managed to forget the wretched woman: all his memories of her were unpleasant. And now once again he would have to remain a prisoner in this garden for hours upon hours ... The thought made him shiver. The war was playing a dirty trick on him in forcing him to return to the prison that had been his childhood, from which he had escaped so long ago. Reality was now resembling the nightmares he regularly had: it was the beginning of a new term in the school dormitory ...

"I couldn't have found you a safer place," the porter repeated.

He tried to reason with himself: his mother was dead, he was an adult, now.

"Is something worrying you?" the porter asked.

Ingrid too was giving him a questioning look.

"No. No. Nothing at all."

"What were you thinking about?" Ingrid asked.

"Nothing."

It was enough to hear Ingrid's voice and to meet her eyes for the past to crumble into dust, with its miserable incidentals: a frivolous mother, an American water ski champion, the white hair and suntanned skin of Monsieur Bailby, and the guests having cocktails down below, by the landing stage. How could all those faded things still cause him any anxiety?

He walked by Ingrid's side in this garden which was now minute, in comparison with what it had been during his childhood: a forest in which he was always afraid of getting lost and never finding his way back to the castle.

"Now I'll show you round the villa ..."

And he was surprised to observe how modest the villa too seemed to him, compared with the castle he remembered in Walter Scott's novels. So that was all it was ...

*

They chose the turret room because of its white walls. On the first floor, the American woman's bedroom was more spacious, but its dark panelling, four-poster bed and Empire furniture gave it a funereal look. Most of the time they used the salon on the ground floor, which had a veranda and opened on to the garden and the sea. One whole wall of this salon was taken up by bookshelves, and they decided to read the books one by one, in the order in which they were arranged on the shelves.

Rigaud avoided the garden. But on sunny days they went down the stone steps to the landing stage. They bathed, and lay on the pontoon from which the water skiers had formerly taken off. Stowed in a garage hollowed out in the rock were the speedboat and the skis. Would they be used again before they rotted?

During the first days, the Provençal porter advised Rigaud and Ingrid not to leave the villa. He made himself responsible for bringing their food. He had gone with Rigaud to the *mairie* in Antibes where, thanks to one of his friends, he had been able to get them a "work permit" specifying that Monsieur and Madame Rigaud were the caretakers of the Villa Saint-Georges, situated in the Boulevard Baudoin in Juan-les-Pins, Alpes-Maritimes. And after all, he had only fulfilled his mission, since the American woman had asked him to keep an eye on the villa in her absence. She had placed it under the protection of the Spanish embassy. Rigaud, who until then had wanted nothing to do with university degrees, official forms, identity papers and good conduct certificates, had asked the porter to get him all the documents that would enable Ingrid to be permanently out of the reach of the French police. So he always carried with him the work permit in the name of Monsieur and Madame Rigaud, and an official letter declaring that the villa was under the direct control of the Spanish embassy in Vichy. As a result, they were in neutral territory and the war no longer concerned them, Ingrid and him.

*

To be on the safe side, he had decided to marry Ingrid in church. The only proof of their civil marriage was Ingrid's false papers in the name of "Madame Rigaud". But there had never been a civil marriage. The religious marriage was celebrated one winter Saturday in the church in Juan-les-Pins. The priest was a friend of the porter, and their witnesses were the porter and the man from the *mairie* who had provided them with their work permit. The wedding breakfast was held in the salon in the villa. The porter had gone down to the cellar to get a bottle of champagne, and they drank to the health of the newlyweds. Rigaud added the certificate of their religious marriage to the papers he already carried with him.

*

They played their part as caretakers conscientiously, and cleaned the villa regularly. They tracked down the slightest speck of dust, polished the furniture, cleaned the windows. Rigaud looked after the speedboat and the water skis. The American woman and Monsieur Bailby would find them intact, if they weren't both too old to use them again after the war. Yes, the war would end. It couldn't go on and on. Everything would come back to normal. That's the law of nature. But they had to stay alive until then. Alive. And not attract attention. Be as inconspicuous as possible. They had definitely given up walking in the deserted streets of Juan-les-Pins. When they bathed, they didn't swim out more than fifty metres from the landing stage, so as not to be seen from the shore.

Ingrid had time to devour all Pierre Benoit's novels, whose red morocco volumes occupied a whole shelf. Each one had an affectionate dedication to the American woman on its fly-leaf. Then she tackled the complete works of Alexandre Dumas, bound in emerald green. She read passages from them to Rigaud, who was repainting the veranda with the last tins of Ripolin found on the black market.

In the evenings they switched on the big wireless in the salon. Every day, at the same time, an announcer with a metallic voice gave the war news in the form of an editorial. Listening to him, Rigaud was convinced that the war would soon be over. This voice had no future, you could tell that from its increasingly metallic tones. It was already a voice from beyond the grave. They would still hear it a little longer, so·long as the war lasted, and then it would fade away from one day to the next.

One winter evening, while they were listening in the semi-darkness of the salon, Rigaud asked Ingrid:

"Doesn't that remind you of something?"

"No."

"It's the voice of the redheaded chap in the dark suit we

met last year in the restaurant ... I'm sure it's him ..."

"Do you think so?"

As the war moved gradually towards its dénouement, the announcer hammered out his phrases more and more emphatically and kept on repeating them. The record was getting stuck in a groove. The voice grew fainter, it got muffled by interference, came back clearly for a few seconds, and then died away again. On the evening of the American landing, a few dozen kilometres from the villa, Ingrid and Rigaud could still just make out the metallic tones of the announcer, lost in the hiss of atmospherics. The voice tried in vain to fight against this storm that was covering it. One last time, before becoming submerged, it broke loose in a hammered-out phrase that was like a cry of hate or an appeal for help.

*

They listened to the announcer at their dinner time, and the voice had lost all reality for them. Now it was no more than a background noise mingled with the music of the orchestras and chansons of those times.

The days, the months, the seasons, the years, went monotonously by, in a kind of eternity. Ingrid and Rigaud barely remembered that they were waiting for something, which must be the end of the war.

Sometimes it forced itself on their attention, and disturbed what Rigaud called their honeymoon. One November evening, some Bersaglieri advanced at the double and took over Juan-les-Pins. A few months later it was the Germans. They built fortifications along the coast and came prowling round the villa. Ingrid and Rigaud had to put out the lights and pretend to be dead.

Once again I went to look at the elephants. You never tire of them.

A slight breeze attenuated the heat. I walked to the perimeter of the zoo, which ran along one of the avenues in the Bois de Vincennes on the Saint-Mandé side, and sat down on a bench. There were tall trees, whose foliage protects you. And an umbrella pine.

After a bit I lay down on the bench. And I wondered whether I would get up of my own accord when the zoo closed, or whether I'd wait until the keeper requested me to move on. I was tempted never to go back to my room in the Dodds Hotel and to let myself slide down the slope which was perhaps my lot, after all: to become a tramp.

I felt fine. Now and then I heard an elephant trumpeting. I didn't take my eyes off the dark-green foliage of the umbrella pine, which stood out against the sky. Juan-les-Pins. I too had been there, a long time before, in the summer when I was twenty-one. But I didn't then know that Ingrid and Rigaud had lived there. I'd met them the previous summer, and as I hadn't seen them since then, I had forgotten them.

It was Cavanaugh who had persuaded me to go to Juan-les-Pins, for a jazz festival. We were not yet fully aware of our vocations as explorers. Cavanaugh was in love with the sister of a negro pianist, and he had got a job as chauffeur to another musician whose name alone was enough to mitigate my depression: Dodo Marmarosa.

I wanted that umbrella pine, between the zoo and Saint-Mandé, to be my mediator and to transmit to me something of the feeling of Juan-les-Pins that summer, when without knowing it I was walking in the tracks of Ingrid and Rigaud. We too went bathing below the casino. And from there, we could see the enormous façade of the Provençal appear at dawn. We weren't staying there but at another, more modest, hotel in a very noisy street.

We lived only at night. I have not the slightest recollection of Juan-les-Pins in the daytime. Except at the fleeting moment when the sun rose. There were so many faces around us that they have all become merged, and I can't make out which one belonged to Dodo Marmarosa. The orchestras played in the pine forest, and that same summer I met Annette. In those days, I thought I was happy.

So I had planned to change hotels every week, and to choose them in the outlying districts of Paris that I had frequented in the old days. From the Dodds, at the Porte Dorée, I had thought of moving to the Fieve Hotel, in the Avenue Simon-Bolivar. I had intended to leave this evening, but I haven't asked for my bill. I, who have travelled so many kilometres over the various continents, I was scared at the thought of taking the métro from the Porte Dorée to the Buttes-Chaumont. After a week at the Porte Dorée, I was afraid of feeling out of my element there. Maybe I'll get up the courage to leave tomorrow morning. But really, I dreaded arriving at the Avenue Simon-Bolivar at dusk, and a too sudden break with the habits I'd got into here at the Porte Dorée.

So I went and had dinner, as I had the previous days, at the café in the Boulevard Soult. Before returning to the hotel, I walked along the perimeter of the zoo as far as the umbrella pine.

I've left the window wide open, I've put out the light and I'm lying on the bed with my arms crossed behind my head. I've become attached to this room, and that's why I'm reluctant to leave. But I'm considering another solution: to make an excursion every day to a different suburb. Then to come back here. If need be, to sleep somewhere else from time to time, with no other luggage than my notes on Ingrid's life. One night at the Fieve, in the Avenue Simon-Bolivar. One night at the Gouin Hotel near the Porte de Clichy . . . But knowing that the Dodds remains my fixed abode, and that this Porte Dorée district is from now on my base. I'd have to pay for my room for several weeks in advance. In that way I'd reassure the proprietor of the Dodds, who must be suspicious of me – I can sense it when we meet in the lobby – because I don't look like an ordinary tourist.

Yes, from time to time spend a night in another district, to dream of the one you've left. In the Fieve Hotel, for instance, I shall lie down on the bed in my room, as I am doing now, and believe I can hear, from a distance, the elephants trumpeting in the zoo. No one will ever be able to find me in any of these places.

*

I was wrong. Yesterday, at the beginning of the afternoon, I had decided to visit the former Colonial Museum. All you have to do when you leave the hotel is cross the square with the fountains, and you come to the low, wrought-iron gate, and the monumental steps leading up to the museum. As I was buying my ticket at the window in the entrance, I thought I recognized, somewhere among the milling crowd of tourists and schoolchildren in the main hall, Ben Smidane's profile. I lost no time in crossing the hall, threading my way between the visitors, and I emerged in a big corner room in which one could admire Marshal Lyautey's study. Someone, behind me, placed his hand on my shoulder:

"Well, Jean, so we're visiting museums?"

I turned round. Ben Smidane. He smiled at me, with an embarrassed smile. He was wearing a very elegant beige summer suit and a sky-blue polo neck.

"What a strange coincidence," I said, urbanely. "I didn't expect to meet you here."

"Nor did I. I thought you'd gone to Rio de Janeiro."

"Well, believe it or not, no."

I hadn't spoken to anyone for something like ten days, and it had taken a considerable effort to utter this one phrase. I wondered whether I would be capable of uttering another. The saliva was drying up in my mouth.

"I knew very well that you weren't in Rio."

He was clearly trying to put me at my ease, and I was grateful to him. No need now to go into any long explanations. I concentrated, and managed to come out with:

"You get tired of everything, even Rio."

"I understand," Ben Smidane said.

But I had a feeling that he didn't understand a thing.

"Jean, I have to talk to you."

He made as if to take me by the arm and lead me away gently, as if he mistrusted my reactions.

"You don't look very confident, Ben. Are you afraid I'll misbehave in Lyautey's study?"

"Not in the least, Jean . . ."

He glanced around him, and then looked at me again. It was as if he was working out the quickest way of tackling me in the middle of the mass of visitors if I suddenly went raving mad.

"Do you like it at the Dodds Hotel?"

He had winked at me. No doubt he was trying to mollify me. But how did he know I was living at the Dodds Hotel?

"Come on, Jean. We absolutely have to talk."

We found ourselves in the square with the fountains.

"Shall we have a drink?" I suggested. "At the zoo cafeteria?"

"Do you go to the zoo?"

I could read his thoughts. For him, I was not in my normal state.

The sun was beating down, and I no longer felt up to walking as far as the zoo.

"I know a café that's nearer, at the corner of the boulevard. There's never anyone in it, and it's very, very cool..."

We were the only customers. He ordered an espresso. So did I.

"Annette sent me," he said.

"Oh yes? How is she?"

I had pretended to be indifferent.

"You must be wondering how I managed to find you? Here."

He held out a crumpled bit of paper on which I read:

Hôtel Gouin? Hôtel de la Jonquière? Quietud's (Rue Berzélius).
Hôtel Fieve.
Hôtel du Point du Jour.
Hôtel Dodds? Hôtel des Bégonias (Rue de Picpus).

"You left it in your study, at the Cité Véron. Annette found it the other evening. And she understood at once."

I had indeed scribbled down these names before my false departure for Rio.

"And you found me right away?"

"No. I've been hanging round the other hotels for four days."

"I feel for you."

"Annette told me she knew all these hotels."

"Yes. We often stayed in them, twenty years ago."

"She asked me to give you this."

On the envelope was written: FOR JEAN, and I recognized one of the qualities I most admired in my wife: the beautiful big handwriting of the illiterate that she was.

Darling,

I miss you. Cavanaugh never leaves me for a second and I have to send you this letter without him knowing. You can trust Smidane and give him a message for me. I want to see you. I'll try to be at the Cité Véron every day at about seven. Phone me. Otherwise, I'll phone you, when I know which hotel you're staying in. I could come and meet you there, like we used to a long time ago. I'll do that without Cavanaugh knowing. I'm not telling anyone that you're still alive. I love you, darling.

Annette

I put the letter in my pocket.

"Have you got a message for her?" Ben Smidane asked me anxiously.

"No."

Ben Smidane's brow furrowed with a studious, childish expression.

"Jean, I find your attitude disconcerting."

He seemed eager to understand, and so deferential towards me – I was older than he, after all – that I felt sorry for him.

"It's very simple. I just feel tired of my life and my job."

He was drinking in my words, and nodding solemnly.

"You're still too young, Ben, to have that feeling. One starts out full of enthusiasm and the spirit of adventure, but after a few years it becomes a job and a routine . . . I don't want to discourage you, though. I'm really the last person to tell anyone what to do."

"You don't realize, Jean . . . We thought you'd disappeared for good . . ."

He hesitated for a few seconds, and then added:

"That you were dead . . ."

"So what?"

He stared at me in consternation.

"You don't know how much Annette loves you . . . The moment she found the bit of paper with the names of the hotels, she decided that life was worth living again . . ."

"And Cavanaugh?"

"She asked me to be sure to tell you that Cavanaugh has never counted for her."

I felt a sudden repugnance at hearing my private life brought up, and embarrassed at seeing Ben Smidane involved in it all.

"At your age, the main thing is to think of yourself and your future, Ben."

He seemed amazed that in such circumstances I should concern myself with him. And yet I would have liked him to talk about the expedition he was planning to the Indian Ocean to search for the wreck of a Dutch galleon, and to share his dreams and illusions with me.

"And you?" he asked. "Are you counting on staying here long?"

He pointed despairingly at the Boulevard Soult outside the café window:

"Then I can tell Annette to come and see you?"

"Tell her not to come just yet . . . She wouldn't find me . . . We mustn't rush things."

He frowned again, in the same studious way as before. He was trying to understand. He didn't want to thwart me.

"Tell her to leave a phone message, or write me a note from time to time. That'll be enough for the time being. Just a message . . . Or a letter . . . Here, at the Dodds Hotel . . . or at the Fieve Hotel . . . Or at the other hotels on the list . . . She knows them all . . ."

"I'll tell her . . ."

"And you, Ben, don't hesitate to come and talk to me about your projects, since you and Annette are the only ones who know I'm still alive . . . But don't let anyone else know."

*

Ben Smidane went off in the direction of the Avenue Daumesnil, and I noticed a phenomenon that doesn't often happen to a man: several women turned round as he passed them.

I was alone again. Naturally, I was expecting to get a message from Annette shortly. But I was certain that she wouldn't turn up unexpectedly. She knew me too well. For twenty years she had found me a good teacher in the art of concealing oneself, of avoiding bores, or of giving people the slip: cupboards you hide in as a last resort, windows you climb out of, back stairs or emergency exits you take at the double, escalators you race down in the wrong direction . . . And all those far-off journeys I had gone on, not to satisfy the curiosity or vocation of an explorer, but to escape. My life had been nothing but evasion. Annette knew that she mustn't rush things: at the slightest alert I was likely to disappear – and this time for good.

But I would have been touched to receive a message from her from time to time, in all these places where we had lived in the old days and which I have now come back to. They haven't changed much. Why, when I was about eighteen, did I leave the centre of Paris and come to these suburban regions? I felt at ease in these districts, I could breathe here. They were a refuge, far away from the bustle of the centre, and a springboard to adventure and to the unknown. You only had to cross a square or walk down an avenue, and Paris was behind you. It was a pleasure to feel myself on the outskirts of the city, with all these lines of escape . . . At night, when all the street lights came on in the Porte de Champerret, the future beckoned to me.

That was what I had tried to explain to Annette, who was amazed that I wanted to live so far out. She had finally understood. Or had pretended to. We had lived in several hotels on the outskirts of Paris. I spent my days vaguely dealing in antiquarian books, but she earned more than I did: two thousand francs a month as a model for L., a famous couture house in the Rue du Faubourg-Saint-Honoré. Her colleagues were all fifteen years older than she was, and didn't forgive her for it.

I remember that the models' dressing room had been relegated to the far end of a back yard. Annette often had to be on duty all day in case a client came to choose a dress. And she had to be on her guard to see that the other models didn't trip her up or scratch her face, and to avoid their stiletto heels, because when the collections were shown she was always the one who wore the wedding dress.

We had lived in the Dodds Hotel for a few weeks, but after all this time I've forgotten the number of our room. The one I'm in today? In any case, my position hasn't changed: I'm lying on the bed, my arms crossed behind the back of my neck, and I'm staring at the ceiling. I used to wait like this on the evenings when she was on duty at the couture house. We would go out to a restaurant and then to the movies. And I can't – incorrigible scribbler that I am – prevent myself from drawing up a rough list of a few places we used to patronize:

ORNANO 43
Chalet Édouard
Brunin-Variétés
Chez Josette de Nice
Delta
La Carlingue
Danube Palace
Petit Fantasio
Restaurant Coquet
Cinéma Montcalm
Haloppé

Just now, going back to the hotel, I had the feeling that I was in a dream. I was going to wake up at the Cité Véron. Annette would still be asleep. I would have returned to real life. I would suddenly remember that we were supposed to be dining with Cavanaugh, Wetzel and Ben Smidane. Or else it would be the fourteenth of July and we would be about to entertain all our friends on the terrace. Then Annette would wake up and, thinking I looked odd, would ask me: "Have you had a nightmare?" I would tell her everything: the false departure for Rio, the journey from Paris to Milan and back, my visit to the flat as if I were now no more than a ghost, my surprise that she should be with Ben Smidane in the locked bedroom, the long afternoons spent at the zoo and around the Porte Dorée, toying with the idea of emigrating to the other peripheral districts she and I had known twenty years ago. And of staying there for good. Annette would say:

"You do have funny dreams, Jeannot."

I pinched my arm. I shook my head. I opened my eyes wide. But I couldn't wake up. I stood motionless in that square, contemplating the water in the fountains and the groups of tourists going into the former Colonial Museum. I wanted to walk to the big café in the Avenue Daumesnil, sit down on the terrace and talk to the people next to me to dispel this feeling of unreality. But that would only further increase my malaise: if I got into conversation with strangers, they would answer me in a different language from mine. Then as a last resort I thought of phoning Annette from my room in the Dodds Hotel. No. I wouldn't be able to get through to her from that room we may perhaps have occupied twenty years ago, the call would be jammed by all those years accumulated one on top of the other. It would be better to ask for a token at the counter of the first café I came to and dial the number from the booth. I abandoned the idea. There too my voice would be so far away that she wouldn't hear it.

I went back to the hotel. I hoped to find a message from Annette there, but there wasn't one. Then I told myself that she would telephone me, and that only the sound of the phone ringing in my room could put an end to my dream. I waited on the bed. Finally I fell asleep, and had a real dream: A summer's night, very hot. I was in a convertible car. I sensed the presence of the driver but couldn't make out his face. We were going from the centre of Paris to the Porte d'Italie district. Now and then it was daytime, we were no longer in the car but walking through little streets like those in Venice or Amsterdam. We crossed an undulating meadow in the town. Then it was night-time again. The car was going slowly down a deserted, badly-lit avenue near the Gare d'Austerlitz. The name: Gare d'Austerlitz, was one of those that accompany you in your sleep and whose resonance and mystery vanish in the morning when you wake up. At last we came to an outer boulevard which sloped gently downwards and where I noticed some palm trees and umbrella pines. A few lights in the windows of the big blocks. Then zones of semi-darkness. The blocks gave place to some warehouses and the perimeter of a stadium ... We turned into a road bordered by a fence and some foliage that hid a railway embankment. And posters advertising the local cinemas were still on the fence. It was such a long time since we'd been in this neighbourhood ...

*

For several days I was on the lookout for a message from Annette. In vain. I left my room as little as possible. One evening, at around seven, I no longer felt the need to wait. Her silence didn't worry me any longer. Perhaps she wanted me to take the first step, but that was unlikely, knowing me as she does.

I went down the hotel stairs and felt as if a weight had been lifted from me. I walked towards the brasserie in the Avenue

Daumesnil where I had decided to have dinner, to change my habits a bit. I began to think about Rigaud. I knew in advance that he wouldn't stop occupying my mind the next day and the following days. If he was alive, and in Paris, I would only have to take the métro and pay him a visit, or even dial eight digits on a telephone to hear his voice. But I didn't think it would be as simple as that.

After dinner I went to the booth in the brasserie to consult the Paris phone book. It was eight years old. I read the long list of Rigauds more carefully than I had the first time. I stopped at a Rigaud whose Christian name wasn't mentioned. 20, Boulevard Soult. 307–75–28. Phone numbers that year still had only seven digits. 307 was the former DORIAN code. I wrote down the address and number.

None of the other Rigauds in the directory seemed to me to be the right one, because of their profession or their address in Paris, or because of the simple indication: M. and Mme Rigaud. What had struck me was the absence of a Christian name, and the address in the Boulevard Soult.

I went out of the brasserie, intending to walk to 20, Boulevard Soult. The sun had disappeared but the sky was still blue. Before the street lights went on, I would take advantage of the moment, the time of day I like best. Not quite daylight. Not yet dark. A feeling of respite and calm comes over you, and that's the moment to lend an ear to echoes that come from afar.

20, Boulevard Soult was a group of blocks in depth, access to which was by a side path. I had been afraid that the name Rigaud might be that of a shop, but I didn't see any at that address. The windows of the block facing the street were not yet lit up. I was reluctant to venture into the side path for fear a resident might ask me what I was doing there. Of course I could always say: "I'm looking for Monsieur Rigaud."

I contented myself with sitting on a bench outside number

20. The street lights came on. I didn't take my eyes off the façade, or the entrance to the side path. On the first floor, one window was now lit up, both halves thrown wide open because of the heat. Someone was living in that little flat, which I imagined consisted of two empty rooms. Rigaud?

I thought of all the travel stories I had found so gripping as an adolescent, and in particular of one book by an Englishman: he described the mirages he had been a victim of in his travels across the desert. On the jacket there was a photo of him dressed as a Bedouin, surrounded by a group of oasis children. And I felt like laughing. Why go so far, when you can have the same experience in Paris, sitting on a bench in the Boulevard Soult? Wasn't that lighted window, behind which I was persuading myself of Rigaud's presence, just as great a mirage as the one that dazzles you in the middle of the desert?

*

The next morning, at about ten, I returned to 20, Boulevard Soult. I went through the front door of the block facing the street. On the left, a little notice was hanging on the door knob of the concierge's lodge. On it was written: "Please enquire at the service station, 16, Boulevard Soult."

Two men were chatting by the petrol pump, one in blue dungarees, the other in a white shirt and grey trousers. The first looked like a Kabyle, the other had white hair combed back, blue eyes and a blotchy complexion. He looked about seventy, and the Kabyle about twenty years younger.

"Can I help you?"

It was the Kabyle in the blue dungarees who had asked this.

"I'm looking for the concierge of number 20."

"That's me."

The white-haired man greeted me with a very brief nod, his cigarette in the corner of his lips.

"I just wanted to ask you something ... About a Monsieur Rigaud ..."

He paused for thought.

"Rigaud? What do you actually want with him?"

He was holding his cigarette between his fingers.

"I'd like to see him."

His fixed look made me feel ill at ease. The Kabyle too was looking at me curiously.

"But he hasn't lived here for ages ..."

He treated me to an indulgent smile, as if he were in the presence of a half-wit.

"The flat hasn't been lived in for at least thirty years ... I don't even know whether Monsieur Rigaud is still alive ..."

The Kabyle in the blue dungarees seemed totally indifferent to Rigaud's fate. Unless he was being tactful and pretending not to listen to us.

"And anyway, I'd rather not know ... I have the impression that the flat belongs to me ... I have the key, and I do the cleaning ..."

"Did you know Monsieur Rigaud?" I asked, my heart beating.

"Yes ... Do you know how long I've been the concierge here?"

He stuck his chest out slightly, looking hard at us one after the other, the Kabyle and me.

"Guess ..."

The Kabyle shrugged his shoulders. I remained silent.

He came nearer, until he was almost pressing himself against me.

"How old would you say I am?"

He was still sticking out his chest, and looking me straight in the eyes.

"Guess ..."

"Sixty."

"I am seventy-five, Monsieur."

He stepped back from us after this revelation, as if to check on the effect he had produced. But the Kabyle remained unmoved. I forced myself to say:

"You really look much younger ... And this Rigaud – when did you know him?"

"In 1942."

"Did he live here alone?"

"No. With a young lady."

"I'd very much like to visit the flat."

"Are you interested in it?"

"It's a real coincidence. I thought a Monsieur Rigaud rented out a flat here...I must have read the name and address wrongly in the advertisements in the paper."

"Do you want to rent a flat in the district?"

"Yes."

"And you'd be interested in Rigaud's flat?"

"Why not?"

"Would you be prepared to rent it until February? I can't let you have it for a shorter period...I always rent it for a minimum of six months..."

"Until February, then."

"Would you pay cash?"

"I would."

The Kabyle in the blue dungarees had offered me a cigarette, before lighting one himself. He was following the conversation absent-mindedly. Perhaps he had long been used to such discussions about the rent of Rigaud's flat.

"I want cash, of course ... How much would you be prepared to pay?"

"Whatever you ask," I said.

He screwed up his blue eyes. He gripped his shirt collar with both hands:

"Mention a figure ..."

*

The flat was on the second floor of the front building and its windows overlooked the Boulevard Soult. A corridor led to the kitchen, a corner of which had been converted into a shower, then to a small empty bedroom whose metal shutters were closed, and finally to what might be called the back bedroom, a fairly spacious room containing twin copper bedsteads pulled close together. Against the opposite wall, a mirrored wardrobe.

The concierge had shut the front door and I was on my own. He had promised to come back later and bring me an oil lamp, because the electricity had been cut off long ago. The phone too. But he would get them reconnected very soon.

The heat was stifling, and I opened the window. The sound of the cars in the boulevard and the sunlight flooding into the room projected this flat into the present. I leaned out of the window. Down below, the cars and lorries were stopping at the traffic lights. A Boulevard Soult different from the one Rigaud and Ingrid had known, and yet the same, on summer evenings or on Sundays, when it was deserted. Yes indeed, I was certain they'd lived here for a time, before they left for Juan-les-Pins. Ingrid had mentioned it the last time I had seen her on her own in Paris. We talked about these outlying districts that I used to frequent at the time – I believe she asked me where I lived – and she told me that she too knew them well, because she'd lived there with her father in the Rue de l'Atlas, near the Buttes-Chaumont. And even with Rigaud, in a small flat. She had got the address wrong. She'd told me Boulevard Davout, instead of Boulevard Soult.

One after the other I opened the wardrobe doors, but there was nothing in it but some hangers. The sunlight reflected in the mirrors made me blink. There was nothing on the walls, whose beige paint was peeling here and there, except a mark above the beds which showed that a painting or a mirror had once hung there. On either side of the beds there was a small table in light-coloured wood covered with a marble slab, like those in hotel rooms. The curtains were wine coloured.

I tried to open the drawer of one of the bedside tables but it resisted. I managed to force the lock with the key to my Cité Véron flat. There was an old brown envelope in the drawer. It was stamped: French State. The address was written in blue ink: M. Rigaud, 3, Rue de Tilsitt, Paris 8ᵉ, but this was crossed out and someone had added in black ink: 20, Boulevard Soult, Paris 12ᵉ. The envelope contained a typewritten sheet.

18 January 1942

NOTICE TO TENANTS

The town house at present let out as flats, in the Place de l'Étoile with an entrance at 3, Rue de Tilsitt, will shortly be sold at auction.

For further information, tenants are requested to apply to Maître Giry, solicitor, 78, Boulevard Malesherbes, and to the State Property Bureau, 9, Rue de la Banque, Paris.

Once again I had the impression that I was in a dream. I held the envelope, I reread the address, I stared and stared at the name: Rigaud, whose letters remained the same. Then I went to the window to make sure that the cars were still going past along the Boulevard Soult, the cars and the Boulevard Soult of today. I felt an urge to phone Annette, just to hear her voice. As I picked up the phone, though, I remembered that it wasn't connected.

There were identical tartan rugs on the twin beds. I sat down on the end of one of them, facing the window. I was holding the envelope. Yes, that was what Ingrid had told me. But you often dream of places and situations someone has told you about, and other details get added. This envelope, for instance. Had it existed in reality? Or was it only an object that was part of my dream? In any case, 3, Rue de Tilsitt had been Rigaud's mother's house, and it was where Rigaud was living when he met Ingrid: she had told me how surprised she'd been when Rigaud had taken her to that flat, where he lived alone, and where he would remain for a few more weeks, and of the sense of security inspired in her by the antique furniture, the carpets that muffled one's footsteps, the paintings, the chandeliers, the panelling, the silk curtains and the conservatory . . .

They hadn't put the lights on in the salon, because of the curfew. They had stood for a few moments at one of the French windows, watching the great patch of the Arc de Triomphe, which was darker than the night, and the Place rendered phosphorescent by the snow.

*

"Were you asleep?"

I hadn't heard him come into the room; he had an oil lamp in his hand. Night had fallen, and I was lying on the bed.

He put the lamp down on the bedside table.

"Are you going to move into the flat right away?"

"I don't know yet."

"I'll give you a pair of sheets, if you like."

The lamp cast shadows on the walls, and I could have imagined that my dream was continuing if I had been alone. But this man's presence seemed very real. And his voice was very clearly audible. I got up.

"You already have some blankets . . ."

He pointed to the tartan rugs on the beds.

"Did they belong to Monsieur Rigaud?" I asked.

"Certainly. They're the only things that were left here, apart from the beds and the wardrobe."

"Then he lived here with a woman?"

"Yes. I remember that they were living here when there was the first air raid over Paris . . . Neither of them wanted to go down to the cellar . . ."

80

He came and leant out of the window by my side. The Boulevard Soult was deserted, and there was a breeze.

"You'll have the telephone at the beginning of next week ... Luckily the water hasn't been cut off, and I've had the shower in the kitchen repaired."

"Do you look after the flat yourself?"

"Yes. I rent it out from time to time, to make a bit of pocket money."

He took a long puff on his cigarette.

"What if Monsieur Rigaud came back?" I asked.

He contemplated the boulevard below with a thoughtful air.

"After the war, I believe they lived in the Midi ... They didn't often come to Paris ... And then, she must have left him ... He was on his own ... For maybe ten years I still saw him from time to time. He used to stay here for a while ... He came to collect his mail ... And then I didn't see him any more ... And I don't think he'll come back."

The grave tone in which he said these last words surprised me. He was staring at a spot below, on the other side of the boulevard.

"People don't come back any more. Haven't you noticed that, Monsieur?"

"I have."

I wanted to ask him what he meant. But I thought better of it.

"By the way, tell me whether you need some sheets?"

"I'm not going to spend the night here yet. All my things are at the Dodds Hotel."

"If you're looking for someone for your move tomorrow, we're here, me and my friend at the garage."

"I have hardly any luggage."

"The shower works well, but there's no soap. I can bring you some up later on. And even some toothpaste..."

"No, I'll spend another night at the hotel . . ."

"As you wish, Monsieur. I must give you the key."

He took a little yellow key out of his trouser pocket and handed it to me.

"Don't lose it."

Was it the same key that Ingrid and Rigaud had used, long ago?

"I'll leave you, now. I'm on duty at the filling station to help my friend out. You'll find me there . . ."

He shook my hand briskly.

"I'll leave you the oil lamp. Don't bother to see me out. I know my way in the dark."

He shut the door gently behind him. I leaned out of the window. I saw him leave the building and slowly pad his way to the service station. I had noticed earlier that he was wearing slippers. His white shirt and beige trousers added a holiday note to the night.

He had joined the Kabyle in the blue dungarees and they were sitting on chairs by the petrol pump. And they must have been smoking peacefully. I too was smoking. I had put out the oil lamp, and the glowing red tip of my cigarette was reflected in the mirror.

There would still be some more beautiful evenings like these, when people would put their chairs out on the pavement to get some fresh air. It was up to me to take advantage of this respite before the first leaves began to fall.

*

It was at the same time of year, one evening at the end of July, that I met Ingrid for the last time. I had gone with Cavanaugh to the Gare des Invalides. He was flying to Brazil, where I was to join him a month later. We were just starting out as professional explorers, and I could never have been able to foresee that one day I would pretend to leave for the same country and then come and take refuge in an hotel in the twelfth arrondissement.

He got into the Orly coach and I found myself alone, not knowing very well what to do with my evening. Annette was spending a few days in Copenhagen with her parents. At that time we were living in a room in the big house that belonged to the Explorers' Club, in Montmartre. I didn't feel like going back there immediately, as it was still light.

I walked at random in a district I hardly knew. I'm shutting my eyes and trying to reconstruct my itinerary. I crossed the Esplanade, walked round the Invalides and came to a zone which, looking back over the years, now seems to me even more deserted than the Boulevard Soult did last Sunday. Wide, shady avenues. The rays of the setting sun lingering on the tops of the buildings.

Someone was walking about ten metres in front of me. There was no one else on the pavement in that avenue running along the side of the École Militaire. Its walls gave the district the appearance of a very distant, very ancient garrison town through which that woman was walking hesitantly, as if she was drunk...

I finally caught her up, and cast a furtive sideways glance at her. I recognized her at once. It was just three years since I had met them for the first time in the Midi, her and Rigaud ... She took not the slightest notice of me. She went on walking, with an absent look, an uncertain gait, and I wondered whether she actually knew where she was going. She must have got lost in that district, along the rectangular avenues which all look alike, and be vainly trying to find some point of reference, a taxi, or a métro station.

I went up closer to her, but she still hadn't noticed that I was there. We walked side by side for a few moments, but I didn't dare speak to her. Finally she turned her head in my direction.

"I believe we know one another," I said.

I felt that she was trying to pull herself together. It must have taken the same kind of effort that you need to force yourself to speak clearly to someone when the phone has just woken you up.

"We know one another?"

She frowned, and contemplated me with her grey eyes.

"You gave me a lift on the Saint-Raphaël road ... I was hitch-hiking ..."

"The Saint-Raphaël road ... ?"

It was as if she was gradually coming up to the surface from the depths.

"Ah yes ... I remember ..."

"You took me to your villa near Pampelonne beach."

I had the impression that I was helping her to get her bearings. She smiled faintly.

"Ah yes ... It wasn't so very long ago ..."

"Three years."

"Three years ... I'd have thought it was less ..."

We were standing still, in the middle of the pavement, facing each other. I was trying to think of something to say to keep her with me. She was going to continue on her way after a few conventional remarks. It was she who broke the silence:

"And you stay in Paris in July? Aren't you going on holiday?"

"No."

"Don't you hitch any more?"

An ironic expression appeared briefly in her eyes.

"If you were hitching here, you wouldn't be likely to find many offers ..."

She pointed to the avenue in front of us.

"It's the desert ..."

I must have been the first person she had spoken to for

several days. And it seems to me, twenty years on, that she was in the same situation as I am this evening, in the Boulevard Soult.

"You might be able to help me to cross this desert," she said.

She smiled at me, and walked more steadily than before.

"How's your husband?"

The moment I said it, this phrase seemed absurd to me.

"He's abroad ..."

She had replied abruptly, and I understood that I wasn't to broach the subject again.

"I've left the Midi ... I've been living in this district for several months ..."

She raised her face to me, and I read anxiety in her grey eyes. And then kindness, and curiosity about me.

"And you? Do you know this district?"

"Not very well."

"Then we're in the same situation."

"Do you live quite near here?"

"Yes. In a big office block, on the top floor ... I have a beautiful view, but there's too much silence in the flat ..."

I said nothing. Night was falling.

"I'm keeping you ..." she said. "You must have something to do ... ?"

"No."

"I'd invite you to have dinner at the flat, but there's nothing to eat."

She hesitated. She frowned.

"We might perhaps try to find a café or a restaurant open ..."

And she looked straight ahead of her at the deserted avenue and the lines of trees, as far as the eye could see, whose foliage had taken on a sombre hue, just after the sun had set.

*

85

Many years later, Cavanaugh rented a minute flat in that district, and he still lives there. He may perhaps be there tonight with Annette. It must be very hot in his two little rooms cluttered with African and Oceanian masks, and Annette will have gone out for a moment to get some fresh air. She'll be walking down the Avenue Duquesne. It's not impossible that she's thinking of me and feeling tempted to come and join me at the Porte Dorée, where Ingrid and Rigaud lived during the air raids. That's the way we are always wandering in the same places at different times and, in spite of the gap between the years, we finally meet.

A restaurant was open in the Avenue de Lowendal, about a hundred metres from where Cavanaugh would later live. I have often passed this restaurant since, and even though because of Cavanaugh I'm now familiar with the district, every time I have had the same feeling that I had with Ingrid that evening, that I was in a different town from Paris, but a town whose name one could not know.

*

"That'll do nicely . . ."

She pointed to one of the tables with an authoritarian gesture which surprised me. I remembered the hesitant way she'd been walking when I had seen her alone, from behind, on the pavement.

An hotel restaurant. A group of Japanese were waiting, rigid, in the middle of the reception hall, with their luggage. The decor of the dining room was resolutely modern: black-lacquered walls, glass tables, leather banquettes, spotlights on the ceiling. We were facing each other and, behind the banquette she was sitting on, phosphorescent fish were swimming round in a big aquarium.

She studied the menu.

"You must eat properly . . . You need to keep up your strength at your age . . ."

"So do you," I said.

"No ... I'm not hungry."

She ordered an hors-d'oeuvre and a main dish for me, and for herself a green salad.

"Are you going to have something to drink?" she asked.

"No."

"Don't you drink alcohol? May I have some?"

She gave me an anxious look, as if I was going to refuse my permission.

"You may," I said.

She raised her head to the maître d'hôtel.

"Well then ... A beer ..."

It was as if she had suddenly decided to do something shameful or forbidden.

"It stops me drinking whisky, or other kinds of alcohol ... I just drink a little beer ..."

She forced herself to smile. She seemed to feel ill at ease with me.

"I don't know what you think," she said, "but I've always thought it wasn't a woman's drink ..."

This time her gaze expressed more than anxiety; distress, rather. And I was so surprised that I couldn't manage to find a comforting word. I finally said:

"I believe you're wrong ... I know a lot of women who drink beer ..."

"Really? You know a lot?"

Her smile and her ironic look reassured me: earlier, when I had taken her by surprise on the pavement, I had wondered whether she was indeed the same person as she had been on the Côte d'Azur. No, she hadn't really changed in three years.

"Tell me what you do. Is it interesting?" she said.

Her salad and beer had been brought. She drank a few mouthfuls, but left the salad untouched. I imagined her alone in her flat, sitting in front of the same salad and the same glass of beer, in the depths of that silence which I still had no experience of at the time, but which is so familiar to me today.

*

I didn't tell her much of the "interesting" things I was doing. A brief reference to my vocation as an explorer and to my imminent departure for Brazil. She too, she disclosed, had spent a few days in Rio de Janeiro. In those days, she must have been my age. She was living in the United States.

I asked her some questions, and I still wonder why she answered them in such detail. I had the definite impression that she felt no kind of self-satisfaction, and that she didn't particularly enjoy talking about herself. She guessed that I was interested, though, and, as she told me several times, "she didn't want me to have a wasted evening."

It does also happen that one evening, because of someone's attentive gaze, you feel a need to communicate to him not your experience, but quite simply some of the various details connected by an invisible thread, a thread which is in danger of breaking and which is called the course of a life.

*

While she was speaking, the fish behind her occasionally pressed their heads against the glass sides of the aquarium. Then they went on tirelessly swimming round in the blue water lit up by a little projector. They had switched off the ceiling spots, to intimate to us that it was very late, and time for us to leave. Only the aquarium light was still on.

At about one in the morning, on the pavement in the avenue, the silence was so profound that you could hear the leaves on the trees rustling with their nocturnal breathing. She took my arm:

"You can see me home . . ."

This time, she was looking for support. It was no longer as

it had been that evening when we were walking down the Rue de la Citadelle when, for the first time in my life, I had had the feeling of being under someone's protection. And yet, after a few steps, once again it was she who was guiding me.

We came to a building with big, dark glass windows. Only two, on the top floor, were lit up.

"I always leave the light on," she said. "It's more cheerful."

She smiled. She was relaxed. But perhaps she was only pretending to take things lightly, to cheer *me* up. This part of the avenue was not planted with trees, but lined with buildings similar to the one she lived in, with all their windows dark. When I used to go to visit Cavanaugh, I couldn't prevent myself from passing that way. I was no longer in Paris, and that avenue led nowhere. Or rather, it was a transit zone to the unknown.

"I must give you my phone number..." She searched her bag, but couldn't find a pen.

"You can tell it to me...I shall remember it..."

I wrote down the number when I was back in Montmartre, in my room at the Explorers' Club. The following days I tried to phone her, several times. There was no answer. In the end I thought I must have remembered the wrong number.

Under the arch over the gate – a wrought-iron gate with opaque glass – she turned round and rested her grey eyes on me. She raised her arm gently and ran the tips of her fingers over my temple and cheek, as if she was for one last time seeking a contact. Then she lowered her arm and the gate closed behind her. That arm suddenly falling and the metallic clank of the gate shutting made me understand that from one moment to another one can lose heart.

I took the oil lamp from the bedside table and once again explored the inside of the wardrobe. Nothing. I picked up the envelope addressed to Rigaud, 3, Rue de Tilsitt, which had been forwarded to 20, Boulevard Soult, and put it in my pocket. Then, lamp in hand, I went down the corridor and into the other bedroom.

I opened the metal shutters, and had great difficulty in folding them back because they had rusted. Then I had no more need of the lamplight: a street lamp just opposite the window filled the room with a white light.

On the left was a small cupboard. The top shelf was empty. Against the wall was a pair of old-fashioned skis. At the bottom of the cupboard, a cheap suitcase. It contained a pair of ski boots and a page torn out of a magazine on which I could make out a few photos. I held the piece of glossy paper up to the light coming from the street lamp and read the text that accompanied the photos:

MEGÈVE HAS NOT BEEN DESERTED. FOR SOME YOUNG MEN A BREAK FROM THEIR ARMY LIFE, FOR OTHERS THEIR LAST HOLIDAYS BEFORE JOINING THE FORCES.

I recognized the twenty-year-old Rigaud in two of the photos. One showed him at the top of a piste, leaning on his ski sticks, the other, on the balcony of a chalet with a woman and a man who was wearing big sunglasses. Underneath the second photo was written: Madame Édouard Bourdet, P. Rigaud, university ski champion 1939, and Andy Embiricos. Moustaches had been pencilled-in on Madame Édouard Bourdet's face, and I was certain that this was the work of Rigaud himself.

I imagined that when he moved from the Rue de Tilsitt to the Boulevard Soult he had taken the skis, the boots and the page from the glossy magazine that dated from the phoney war. One evening, in this room where he had taken refuge with Ingrid – the evening of the first air raid over Paris, but neither of them went down to the cellar – he must have contemplated these accessories with stupefaction, as relics of a previous life – that of a dutiful young man. The world he had grown up in and belonged to until he was twenty must have seemed so far-off and so absurd that while waiting for the end of the raid, he had absent-mindedly drawn moustaches on Madame Bourdet.

*

Before shutting the flat door, I checked to see whether the yellow key the concierge had given me was still in my pocket. Then I went down the stairs in semi-darkness, because I hadn't been able to find the light switch.

Down on the boulevard, the night was a little cooler than usual. Outside the service station, the Kabyle in the blue dungarees was sitting on a chair and smoking. He waved to me.

"Are you on your own?" I asked.

"He went to get some sleep. He's going to take over later."

"Do you work all night?"

"All night."

"Even in the summer?"

"Yes. It doesn't bother me. I don't like sleeping."

"If you ever need me," I said, "I could stand in for you

whenever you like. I live in the district now, and I've nothing else to do."

I sat down on the chair opposite him.

"Would you like some coffee?" he said.

"With pleasure."

He went into the office and came back with two cups of coffee.

"I put a lump of sugar in. Is that all right?

We were now sitting on our chairs and sipping our coffee.

"Do you like the flat?"

"Very much," I said.

"I rented it from my friend, too, for three months, before I found a studio flat in the neighbourhood."

"And the flat was empty, as it is now?"

"All that was left was an old pair of skis in a cupboard."

"They're still there," I told him. "And your friend has no idea where to find the former owner?"

"He may be dead, you know."

He put his coffee cup down on the pavement by his feet.

"If he isn't dead, he might get in touch all the same," I said.

He smiled at me with a shrug of the shoulders. We remained silent for a few moments. He seemed thoughtful.

"In any case," he said, "he was a man who must have liked winter sports..."

*

Back at the hotel, I opened the folder containing my notes on Ingrid's life, and added the page torn out of the magazine and the envelope addressed to Rigaud. Yes, 3, Rue de Tilsitt had indeed been where Madame Paul Rigaud had lived. I had written it down on a bit of paper after checking in an old directory. During the few days that Ingrid had lived with Rigaud in the Rue de Tilsitt it had been snowing in Paris, and they hadn't left the flat. Through the big windows in the salon they looked at the snow covering the Place and the avenues all around, and enveloping the city in a blanket of silence, softness and sleep.

*

I woke up at about noon, and again hoped to get a message or a phone call from Annette before the end of the day. I went and had breakfast in the café on the other side of the square with the fountains. When I got back, I told the *patron* that I would be in my room until the evening, so that he wouldn't forget to come and fetch me if my wife phoned.

I've thrown open both halves of the window. A radiant summer's day. Nothing like the heatwave of the previous days. A group of children guided by monitors is making its way towards the former Colonial Museum. They stop, and surround the ice cream seller. The water in the fountains is sparkling in the sunlight, and I have no difficulty in transporting myself from this peaceful July afternoon where I am at the moment to the far-off winter when Ingrid met Rigaud for the first time. There's no frontier between the seasons any more, or between the past and the present.

*

It was one of the last days in November. As usual, she had left the dancing class at the Châtelet Theatre in the late afternoon. She hadn't much time now to get back to her father in the hotel in the Boulevard Ornano where they had been living since the beginning of the autumn: that evening the curfew was going to start at six throughout the arrondissement, because there had been an attack the day before on some German soldiers in the Rue Championnet.

She had earned some money for the first time in her life by

93

dancing in the chorus, with some of her classmates, for the whole of the previous week, in a production of *Vienna Waltzes* at the Châtelet. A fee of fifty francs. Night was already falling, and she crossed the square to get to the entrance to the métro. Why did she feel so discouraged this evening at the prospect of going home to her father? Doctor Jougan had gone to live in Montepellier and he wouldn't be able to help her father any more, as he had so far done by employing him in his clinic in Auteuil. He had suggested that her father should join him in Montpellier, in the unoccupied zone, but he would have had to cross the demarcation line illegally . . . Of course, the doctor had asked the other people in the Auteuil clinic to look after her father, but they had neither Doctor Jougan's generosity nor his courage: they were afraid it might be discovered that an Austrian, registered as a Jew, was working clandestinely in their clinic . . .

She felt suffocated in the métro carriage, crammed up against all the other passengers. It was more crowded than usual, no doubt because of the six o'clock curfew. At the Strasbourg-Saint-Denis station, so many people got in that the doors wouldn't shut. She ought to have taken a bicycle-taxi with the fifty francs from *Vienna Waltzes*. Or even a horse-drawn cab. In the time it took to get to the Boulevard Ornano, she would have imagined that the war was over and that she was travelling through a different town in a happier period than this one, the period of *Vienna Waltzes*, for instance.

*

She didn't get out at Simplon as she usually did, but at Barbès-Rochechouart. It was half past five. She preferred to walk to the hotel in the fresh air.

There were groups of German soldiers and French policemen at the entrance to the Boulevard Barbès, as if it was a frontier post. She had a presentiment that if she went down the boulevard like the other people going home to the eighteenth arrondissement, the frontier would close behind her for ever.

She walked down the Boulevard Rochechouart on the left-hand pavement, which was in the ninth arrondissement. From time to time she glanced at the opposite pavement which marked the limit of the curfew and where it was darker, even though it wasn't six yet: still fifteen minutes before the frontier closed, and if she didn't cross it before then she wouldn't be able to get back to her father at the hotel. The métro stations in the district would also close at six. In the Place Pigalle, another frontier post. German soldiers were surrounding a lorry. But she walked straight on, on the same pavement, along the Boulevard de Clichy. Now only ten minutes. Place Blanche. There, she stopped for a few moments. She was just about to cross the Place and the frontier, she took three steps, and stopped again. She walked back on the pavement in the Place Blanche, on the ninth arrondissement side. Now only five minutes. She mustn't give way to the impulse to let herself be sucked into the darkness over on the other side. She must stick to the ninth arrondissement pavement. She walked up and down outside the Café des Palmiers and the chemist's in the Place Blanche. She forced herself not to think of anything, and especially not of her father. She counted. Twenty-three, twenty-four, twenty-six, twenty-seven ... Six o'clock. Five past six. Ten past six. There. It was over.

*

She must go on walking straight ahead on the same pavement, and she must avoid looking over on to the other side where the curfew zone began. She quickened her pace as if she were hurrying over a narrow gangway and all the time afraid of toppling over into the void. She hugged the walls of the buildings and of the Lycée Jules-Ferry, where she had still been a pupil the year before.

When she had crossed the Place de Clichy, she finally turned her back on the eighteenth arrondissement. She was leaving it behind her, that district now forever drowned in the curfew. It was as if she had jumped from a sinking ship just in time. She didn't want to think about her father because she still felt too close to that dark, silent zone from which no one would ever be able to escape now. For her part, she had only just managed it.

She no longer felt the sense of suffocation that had come over her in the métro, and a little while before at the Barbès-Rochechouart crossroads at the sight of the motionless soldiers and policemen. It seemed to her that the avenue opening out in front of her was a big forest path which led, farther on, to the west, to the sea whose spray the wind was already blowing in her face.

*

Just as she reached the Étoile, it began to rain. She sheltered under a porch in the Rue de Tilsitt. On the ground floor of the next building there was a teashop called Le Rendez-vous. She hesitated a long time before going in, because of her sports coat and old pullover.

She sat down at a table in the back. There were not many customers that evening. She jumped: the pianist on the other side of the room was playing one of the tunes from *Vienna Waltzes*. A waitress brought her a cup of chocolate and a macaroon and gave her an odd look. She suddenly wondered whether she had a right to be there. Perhaps this teashop was forbidden to "unaccompanied minors". Why did that expression come to her mind? Unaccompanied minors. She was sixteen, but she looked twenty. She tried to bite into the macaroon but it was hard, and the chocolate was a very pale, almost mauve colour. It really didn't taste of chocolate. Would the fifty francs she'd earned from *Vienna Waltzes* be enough to pay the bill?

When the teashop closed, she would find herself outside, in the rain. And she would have to look for somewhere to shelter until midnight. And after the curfew? Panic gripped her. She hadn't thought of that when she was walking along, hugging the walls to escape the other curfew, the six o'clock one. She had noticed a couple of young men at a table near hers. One was wearing a light grey suit. His chubby face was in contrast to the severity of his gaze and his thin-lipped mouth. What made his gaze severe and staring was a big patch over his right eye. His blond hair was combed backwards. The other was dark, and wearing a shabby tweed jacket. They were talking in low voices. Her eyes had met those of the dark one. The other snapped open a gold-plated cigarette case, put a cigarette between his lips and lit it with a lighter that was also gold-plated. It looked as if he was explaining something to the dark one. Occasionally he raised his voice, but the piano music drowned his words. The dark one listened, and nodded from time to time. She met his eyes again, and he smiled at her.

*

The fair-haired man in the light grey suit waved a nonchalant goodbye to the other, and went out. The dark one stayed alone at the table. The pianist was still playing the tune from *Vienna Waltzes*. She was afraid that closing time had come.

Everything around her began to swim. She tried to stop her nervous trembling. She gripped the edge of the table and kept her eyes fixed on the cup of chocolate and the macaroon she hadn't been able to eat.

The dark young man stood up and went over to her.

"You look as if you're not feeling well . . ."

He helped her to stand up. Outside, they took a few steps

in the rain and she felt better. He was holding her arm.

"I didn't go home . . . In the eighteenth arrondissement . . . because of the curfew . . ."

She had said these words very quickly, as if she wanted to get rid of a great weight. Suddenly she began to cry. He pressed her arm.

"I live very near here . . . You can come home with me . . ."

They walked round the bend in the road. It was just as dark as it had been earlier when she was on the border of the curfew, and fighting with all her strength against the impulse to leave the ninth arrondissement pavement. They crossed an avenue whose dimmed street lamps gave out a blue light.

"What do you do? Is it interesting?"

He had asked her this in affectionate tones, to give her confidence. She had stopped crying, but she felt the tears trickling over her chin.

"I'm a dancer."

*

She felt intimidated as they went through the gate and crossed the courtyard of one of the big town houses round the Place de l'Étoile. He opened a front door on the second floor and stood aside to let her go in first.

Lighted lamps and chandeliers. The curtains were drawn to conceal the lights. She had never seen such enormous rooms or such high ceilings. They crossed a hall, and then a bedroom whose walls were covered with shelves full of old books. A log fire in the salon was almost out. He told her to take off her coat and sit on the settee. At the far end of the salon there was a conservatory under a big glazed rotunda.

"You can phone home."

He put the phone down beside her on the settee. She hesitated for a moment. You can phone home. She remembered the number all right: MONTMARTRE 33–83, the number of the café on the ground floor of the hotel. The *patron* would answer, unless he'd closed the café because of the curfew. With a hesitant finger, she dialled the number. He was bending over the fire, poking a log.

"Could you leave a message for Doctor Teyrsen?"

She had to repeat the name several times.

"The doctor who lives in the hotel ... Yes ... From his daughter ... Tell him that everything is all right ..."

She hung up, very quickly. He went and sat beside her on the settee.

"You live in an hotel?"

"Yes. With my father."

Their two rooms could easily have fitted into a corner of the salon. She visualized the front door of the hotel, and the red-carpeted spiral staircase that led up steeply to the first floor. On the right of the corridor, rooms 3 and 5. And this salon where she now was, with its silk curtains, its panelling, its chandelier, its paintings and conservatory ... She wondered whether she was in the same town or whether she was dreaming, as she had been earlier in the métro, when she had imagined herself returning to the Boulevard Ornano in a horse-drawn cab. And yet there were no more than twelve métro stations between this place and the Boulevard Ornano.

"And you? Do you live here alone?"

He shrugged his shoulders ruefully, as if he were apologizing.

Something suddenly gave her confidence. She noticed, when he made a rather too abrupt gesture as he removed the phone from the settee, that the lining of his tweed jacket was torn. And his big shoes. One of them didn't even have a lace.

*

99

They had dinner in the kitchen, at the far end of the flat. But there wasn't very much to eat. Then they went back to the salon, and he said:

"You'll have to stay the night here."

He led her into the next room. In the over-bright light of the chandelier there was a four-poster bed with wooden carvings and a silk canopy.

"This was my mother's room ..."

He noticed that she was surprised by the four-poster bed and by the room, which was almost as big as the salon.

"Doesn't she live here any more?"

"She's dead."

The bluntness of this reply took her aback. He smiled at her.

"My parents have been dead for quite some time."

He walked round the room, as if on a tour of inspection.

"I don't think you'll feel very comfortable here ... It would be better for you to sleep in the library ..."

She had lowered her head, and couldn't take her eyes off that big shoe without a lace that made such a strong contrast with the four-poster bed, the chandelier, the panelling and the silks.

*

In the book-lined room they had crossed earlier, after the hall, he pointed to the divan:

"I must give you some sheets."

Very fine voile sheets, pinkish beige and edged with lace. He had also brought her a tartan wool blanket and a little pillow without a pillow slip.

"This is all I could find."

He seemed to be apologizing.

She helped him make the bed.

"I hope you won't be cold . . . They've turned the heating off . . ."

She had sat down on the edge of the divan, and he in the old leather armchair in the corner of the library.

"So you're a dancer?"

He didn't really seem to believe it. He was giving her an amused look.

"Yes. A dancer at the Châtelet. I was in the cast of *Vienna Waltzes*."

She had adopted a haughty tone.

"I've never been to the Châtelet . . . But I'll come and see you . . ."

"Unfortunately, I don't know whether I'll be able to go on working . . ."

"Why not?"

"Because my father and I are in trouble."

*

She had hesitated to tell him about her situation, but the tweed jacket with the torn lining and the shoe without a lace had encouraged her. And then, he often used slang words that didn't go with the refinement and luxury of the flat. She had even begun to wonder whether he really lived there. But on one of the shelves in the library there was a photo of him much younger, with a very elegant woman who must have been his mother.

He left her, wishing her a good night, and saying that at breakfast the next day she would be able to drink some real coffee. Then she was alone in the room, amazed to find herself on that divan. She didn't put the light out. If she felt she was falling asleep she would put it out, but not just yet. She was afraid of the dark because of the curfew that evening in the eighteenth arrondissement, the dark that reminded her of her father and the hotel in the Boulevard Ornano. How reassuring it was to contemplate the bookshelves, the opalescent lamp on the little table, the silk curtains, the big Louis XV bureau over by the windows, and to feel the fresh lightness of the voile sheets . . . She hadn't told him the truth. In the first place she had pretended that she was nineteen. And then, she wasn't really a dancer at the Châtelet. Next, she had said that her father was an Austrian doctor who had emigrated to France before the war, and that he worked in a clinic in Auteuil. She hadn't touched on the root of the problem. She had added that they were only living in the hotel temporarily, because her father was looking for another flat. She hadn't admitted, either, that she had purposely let the time of the curfew go by so as not to go back to the Boulevard Ornano. In other times, no one would have attached much importance to this fact, it would even have seemed quite normal for a girl of her age, and would simply have been seen as an escapade.

*

The next day, she didn't go back to the hotel in the Boulevard Ornano. She again phoned MONTMARTRE 33-83. Doctor Teyrsen's daughter. They must leave a message for the doctor: "Tell him not to worry." But the *patron* of the café and the hotel, whose voice Ingrid recognized, replied that her father was expecting this phone call and that he'd go and fetch him from his room. Then she hung up.

Another day went by. Then another. They didn't leave the flat, she and Rigaud, except to go and have dinner in a nearby black market restaurant in the Rue d'Armaillé. They went to the cinema in the Champs-Élysées. The film was *Remorques*. A few more days went by and she didn't phone MONTMARTRE 33-83 again. December. Winter was beginning. The Resistance mounted more attacks, and this time the curfew was imposed at half past five for a week. The whole town was plunged into darkness, cold and silence. You had to go to ground wherever you happened to be, keep your head down as far as possible, and wait. She didn't ever want to leave Rigaud, and the Boulevard Ornano seemed so far away . . .

*

At the end of the curfew week, Rigaud told her that he had to leave the flat because the building was going to be sold. It belonged to a Jew who had taken refuge abroad and whose property had been sequestrated. But he had found another flat near the Vincennes zoo and, if she liked, he could take her there.

*

One evening they had dinner in the restaurant in the Rue d'Armaillé with the fair-haired young man in the light grey suit and the patch over his eye. Ingrid instinctively disliked and distrusted him. And yet he was very affable, and asked her questions about the Châtelet where she pretended she had been a dancer. He called Rigaud *tu*. They had known each other as children, in the lower forms of their Passy boarding school, and he would have liked to reminisce about this period of their life at greater length, if Rigaud hadn't said curtly:

"That's enough about that . . . It brings back unpleasant memories . . ."

The blond young man made a lot of money out of black market deals. He was in contact with a Russian who had offices in a town house in the Avenue Hoche, and with a whole lot of other "interesting" people whom he would introduce to Rigaud.

"There's no point," Rigaud had said. "I'm thinking of leaving Paris . . ."

And the conversation had come back to the flat. The young man was offering to buy all its furniture and paintings before Rigaud left. He had mentioned them to one of his "connec-

103

tions", whose agent he would be. He prided himself on being a connoisseur of antique furniture. He acted the man of the world and mentioned with feigned indifference that one of his ancestors had been a Marshal of the Empire. Rigaud simply called him Pacheco. When he had introduced himself to Ingrid, he had said, with a slight bow of the head: Philippe de Pacheco.

*

The next afternoon there was a ring at the flat door. A youth in a lumber-jacket announced that Pacheco had sent him with a van and the removal men. He had taken the liberty of opening the street gates and parking the van in the courtyard, if no one had any objection. As the removal men began collecting the furniture, Ingrid and Rigaud took refuge at the far end of the salon, in the conservatory. But after a few moments they decided they would rather go out. A van covered by a tarpaulin was waiting by the steps.

They walked down the gently-sloping Avenue de Wagram. The snow had melted on the pavements, and a pale winter sun was breaking through the clouds. Rigaud told her that Pacheco was going to bring him the money from the sale of the furniture that evening, and that they could move into their new flat at once. She asked him whether he was sorry to leave this area. No. He had no regrets, and he was even glad not to be staying there.

They had reached the Place des Ternes. Suddenly she felt an impulse: to carry straight on to Montmartre and return to the hotel in the Boulevard Ornano, to retrace, in the opposite direction, the steps she had taken the other evening to get away from the curfew zone. She sat down on a bench. Once again she began to tremble.

"What's the matter?"

"Nothing. It'll pass."

They turned back. He put his arm round her shoulder, and gradually she felt reassured at the thought of going back with him up the Avenue de Wagram towards the Étoile.

*

There was now a second van with a tarpaulin parked beside the other by the steps. Several men were loading the Louis XV bureau, a console table and a chandelier. The youth in the lumber-jacket was supervising the removal men's comings and goings.

"Will you be much longer?" Rigaud asked him.

He replied in a sing-song voice:

"No ... no ... We've nearly finished ... We aren't taking this stuff very far ... Avenue Hoche ..."

That was no doubt the town house Pacheco had mentioned, where the Russian had his "offices".

"There's plenty of it ..."

He shifted from one leg to the other and gave them a condescending look.

Everything had gone from the library but the books on the shelves. They had even taken the curtains. There was not a single piece of furniture left in the big salon, the chandelier had been taken down and the carpet rolled up. Only the paintings were still in place. They shut themselves in a boudoir next to the salon, from which the men had forgotten to take the divan.

*

At about seven, Pacheco put in an appearance, accompanied by a man of about fifty who had a fat face and silvery hair and who was wearing a fur-lined coat. Pacheco introduced him as the Marquis de W. He was the one who was interested in the paintings. He wanted to see them and choose some, or perhaps even take them all. The youth in the lumber-jacket had joined them and seemed to know the self-styled marquis very well, as he said to him in his sing-song voice:

"Have you come to see the stuff?"

In the salon, the Marquis de W., who hadn't taken off his fur-lined coat, inspected the paintings one by one. The youth in the lumber-jacket stood behind him, and after a moment said:

"Do we take it down?"

And on a nod from the Marquis de W., he took the painting down and propped it up against the wall. At the end of this inspection, all the paintings had been taken down. Ingrid and Rigaud stayed in the background. The Marquis de W. turned to Pacheco:

"Does your friend still agree the price we fixed?"

"He does."

Rigaud was then obliged to join them, and the Marquis de W. said to him:

"I'm taking all the paintings. I'd have been quite willing to buy the furniture, but I don't need it."

"We've already found a buyer," Pacheco said.

Rigaud had imperceptibly drifted away from them. Ingrid was still at the back of the salon, near the door. He went over to her. He looked at the three men standing in the middle of the empty room, the one in his fur-lined coat which seemed as new as his title, Pacheco in a raincoat with its collar turned down, and the youngest one in his lumber-jacket. They looked like burglars who had just finished the job but who had nothing to fear, and could afford to linger at the scene of their misdeeds. The light streamed down from a naked bulb hanging from the ceiling in the place of the chandelier.

*

The Marquis de W. and the youth in the lumber-jacket left the flat first and started down the stairs. Pacheco handed Rigaud a cardboard shoe box:

"Here ... You can check that it's all there ... Will you come and see us out?"

Rigaud, shoe box in hand, preceded Ingrid down the stairs. They all found themselves on the steps outside the house. Night had fallen, and it was snowing slightly. The larger of the two vans began to drive off, and had difficulty in turning into the Rue de Tilsitt. Then the other van followed.

"Maybe we could have dinner together," Pacheco suggested.

Rigaud nodded. Ingrid was keeping in the background.

"You must be my guests," said the Marquis de W.

"Why don't we go to the restaurant where we were the other evening?" said Pacheco.

"Where was it?" the Marquis de W. asked.

"In the Rue d'Armaillé. Chez Moitry."

"Good idea," said the Marquis de W. Then, turning to Rigaud:

"I gather the house has been sequestrated, and is on the market. Maybe you can give me some tips."

The youth in the lumber-jacket kept by the Marquis de W.'s side like a bodyguard. It was snowing harder, now.

"See you chez Moitry in an hour," said Rigaud. "I must just make a last tour of inspection upstairs."

He joined Ingrid on the steps. They watched the others cross the courtyard and go through the gate. With a chauffeur's gesture, the youth in the lumber-jacket opened one of the doors of a black saloon parked outside.

The Marquis de W. and Pacheco got in. It was snowing harder all the time, and the car disappeared round the corner in the Rue de Tilsitt.

*

Rigaud had taken a bag into the salon. Under the harsh light of the bulb hanging from the ceiling, he packed a few sweaters, a pair of trousers and the shoe box full of bank-notes that Pacheco had given him. Ingrid had no other clothes than the ones she was wearing. He closed the bag.

"Must we really have dinner with them?" Ingrid asked.

"No ... no ... I don't trust those people ..."

She was relieved. She too felt ill at ease in their presence.

"We'll go to the other flat right away ..."

When he went out of the salon he left the light on. As he was shutting the flat door he said to Ingrid, who was on the landing:

"Wait here a moment ..."

He soon came back with a pair of skis, and some big boots which he put in the bag.

"They're souvenirs ..."

On the stairs, each took one handle of the bag. Rigaud had put the skis over his shoulder.

*

It was still snowing. The pavement was covered in a white layer which gleamed in the darkness. The Place was deserted, and they sank up to their ankles in the snow. The Arc de Triomphe stood out clearly in the moonlight.

"It's a pity you haven't got any skis," said Rigaud. "We could have skied there ..."

They went down the steps to the métro. There were not so many people in the carriage as there had been the other evening between Châtelet and Barbès-Rochechouart. Ingrid sat down near the doors and held the bag on her knees. Rigaud remained standing, because of the skis. The other passengers looked at him curiously. And in the end, he didn't even pay attention to the successive stops: Marbeuf, Concorde, Palais-Royal, Louvre ... He tightened his grasp on the skis against his shoulder and imagined himself once again, as he had been the previous year, in the ski-lift taking him all the way up to Rochebrune.

*

The train stopped at Nation. The line didn't go any farther. Rigaud and Ingrid had gone past Bastille, where they ought to have changed for the Porte Dorée.

They came out of the métro into a big snowfield. Neither of them knew the district. Maybe there was a street that would be a short cut to 20, Boulevard Soult? They decided to go the safest way: along the Cours de Vincennes.

They hugged the façades of the buildings, where the snow wasn't so deep. Rigaud was carrying his skis over his shoulder, and the bag in his left hand. Ingrid kept her hands in her coat pockets, because she was cold.

They saw a sledge going by on the pavement, harnessed to a black horse. Maybe the silence, the full moon and the phosphorescent snow were creating mirages. The sledge advanced slowly, no faster than a hearse. Rigaud put his skis down on the ground and ran after it, calling to the driver, who stopped his horse.

He agreed to take them to 20, Boulevard Soult. Usually he drove a cab, but during the fortnight that Paris had been snowbound he had used this sledge which he had discovered in a shed in Saint-Mandé, near where he lived. He was wearing a big lumber-jacket and a fisherman's cap.

They glided along the Cours de Vincennes. Rigaud's skis were tied on to the back of the sledge. With an abrupt movement of his arm, the cabbie whipped his horse whenever it slowed to a walk. But as they approached the Porte de Vincennes, its trot became faster. They no longer knew what town they were in or what countryside they were travelling through. The sledge cut through several little streets to get to the Boulevard Soult. It was a silent, deserted mountain village during Midnight Mass. Ingrid nestled down in the hollow of Rigaud's shoulder.

I left my hotel room in the late morning without having received a message from Annette, and went back to the flat. I put the yellow key in the lock and had difficulty in opening the door.

I came upon the concierge in the end bedroom, putting sheets on the twin beds.

"You needn't have bothered," I said. "I'll do it myself."

He straightened up.

"But it's no trouble, Monsieur. After all, you aren't going to camp here, are you?"

He looked at me reproachfully.

"And this afternoon I'll run the vacuum cleaner over the place. There's far too much dust . . ."

"You think so?"

It had been accumulating for a long time. I tried to work out how long it had been since Ingrid and Rigaud left.

"I'll get rid of those skis in the cupboard, and those old boots . . ."

"No. They must stay where they belong."

He seemed surprised at my determination.

"Just imagine if that Monsieur Rigaud came back and found his skis gone . . ."

He shrugged his shoulders.

"He'll never come back."

I helped him tuck in the sheets. We had to separate the twin beds, which had been pushed together.

"They're going to reconnect the phone at the beginning of next week," he told me. "And the electricity this afternoon."

So everything was for the best. I would phone Annette and tell her to come and join me here. We would live together in this flat. She'd be surprised at first, but she would finally understand, as she had finally understood so many things when we first knew one another.

*

We went out on to the Boulevard Soult and walked to the service station. The Kabyle in the blue dungarees shook my hand.

"I'll leave you to your shift," he said to the concierge.

"Will you keep me company for a bit?" the concierge asked me.

"With pleasure."

We sat down on the chairs by the petrol pump. We stayed in the sun. It didn't overwhelm us as it had the previous days, but enveloped us in a gentle warmth and an orange-coloured light.

"It's already autumn," said the concierge. And he pointed to the foot of a tree, where a few dead leaves were stuck in the wire cage round its trunk.

"I must remember to check the radiators in your flat. Otherwise you won't have any proper heating this winter."

"There's still time," I said.

"Not so much . . . It goes fast . . . As from September, the days get shorter . . ."

"I don't know whether I shall still be there this winter."

Yes, all of a sudden the prospect of staying in this district during the winter chilled my heart. In the summer, you're a tourist like any other, in a town that is also on holiday. You aren't in any way committed. But in the winter ... And the thought that Annette would agree to share my life at the Porte Dorée didn't make me feel any more cheerful. My goodness, where and how was I going to spend the winter?

"Is something bothering you?" the concierge asked.

"No."

He stood up.

"I have to go and do some shopping for my dinner. Can you stay here? If by any chance anyone wants some petrol, will you be able to work the pump?"

"There can't be much magic about it," I said.

*

An old navy-blue English car had been standing for a few moments opposite the petrol station on the other side of the road. I thought I recognized Annette's car. Yes. It was indeed Annette's car. But I couldn't see who was driving.

The car made a wide U-turn on the deserted boulevard and pulled up outside the service station. Ben Smidane. He put his head out of the window.

"Jean ... It took me a long time to find you ... I've been watching you for the last ten minutes to make quite sure that it was you..."

He gave me a rather nervous smile.

"Shall I fill her up?" I asked.

And without even giving him time to reply, I unhooked the pipe and began to fill the tank.

"You've found a new job, then?"

His tone was jocular, but he couldn't manage to conceal his concern. He got out of the car and stood squarely in front of me.

"Annette sent me ... You must give her some sign of life, Jean ..."

I hooked the pipe slowly back on to the pump.

"She's very worried about you."

"She certainly shouldn't be."

"She didn't want to phone you because she's afraid . . ."

"Afraid of what?"

I was automatically wiping the windscreen with a rag I'd found on the petrol pump.

"She's afraid you're going to involve her in an adventure that leads nowhere . . . Those are her own words . . . She doesn't want to come and see you here . . . She told me that she isn't twenty any more . . ."

*

The concierge was slowly coming towards us on the pavement, carrying his shopping bag. I introduced Ben Smidane to him. Then Ben got back behind the wheel and signed to me to come and sit beside him. He drove off. There were vestiges of Annette's scent in the car.

"It would be so much simpler if I were to take you back to your wife now."

We were driving very slowly in the direction of the Porte Dorée.

"Not just yet," I said. "I must stay here for a few more days."

"Why?"

"To give me time to finish my Memoirs."

"Are you writing your Memoirs?"

I could see that he didn't believe me. And yet I was telling the truth.

"Not really Memoirs," I said. "But almost."

We had reached the square with the fountains and were driving past the former Colonial Museum.

"I've been making notes over a long period, and now I'm trying to turn them into a book."

"And why couldn't you write your book at home, at the Cité Véron, with Annette?"

"I need a certain atmosphere . . ."

But I didn't feel like giving him any sort of explanation.

"Listen, Jean . . . I'm leaving tomorrow for the Indian Ocean . . . I'm going to be there for several months . . . I won't be able to act as a go-between for you and Annette any longer . . . It would be a real shame if you were to make a definite break . . ."

"You're lucky to be still at an age to go away . . ."

This had escaped me, just like that. I too would have liked to go away instead of going around in circles on the periphery of this town like someone who can no longer find any emergency exits. I so often have the same dream: I'm on the landing stage, waiting to take off, my water skis on my feet, I'm gripping the rope and waiting for the speedboat to move off and tow me over the water at top speed. But it doesn't move.

He left me outside the hotel.

"Jean, will you promise me to phone her as soon as possible?"

"As soon as they've reconnected the phone in the flat."

He didn't know what to make of my reply.

"And you," I said, "I wish you success in your treasure hunt in the Indian Ocean."

*

Back in my room, I once again looked through my notes. In the summer before the war, and sometimes even during the first year of the Occupation, when Ingrid came out of the Lycée Jules-Ferry she took the métro to Église d'Auteuil and went and fetched her father from Doctor Jougan's clinic. It was in a little street between the Avenue de Versailles and the Seine.

He always left the clinic at about half past seven. She used to walk round the block while she was waiting for him. She would come back to the street and see him outside the clinic door, waving to her.

They would walk through this calm, almost rural district, where they could hear the bells of Sainte-Périne or Notre-Dame-d'Auteuil. And they would go and have dinner in a restaurant which I couldn't find the other evening, when I was walking in that vicinity, in the traces of Doctor Teyrsen and his daughter.

I came across the old newspaper cutting dating from the winter when Ingrid had met Rigaud. Ingrid had given it to me the last time I saw her. While we were having dinner she had begun to tell me about all that period, and she'd taken a crocodile wallet out of her bag, and out of the wallet a carefully-folded cutting she had kept with her over all those years. I remember that at that moment she fell silent, and looked at me with a strange expression, as if she wanted to transfer to me a burden that had long weighed on her, or as if she guessed that I too, later, would go looking for her.

It was a tiny paragraph among the other advertisements, the situations wanted and vacant, the property and commercial transactions column:

"Missing: Ingrid Teyrsen, sixteen, 1m60, oval face, grey eyes, brown sports coat, light blue pullover, beige skirt and hat, black casual shoes. All information to M. Teyrsen, 39*bis*, Boulevard Ornano, Paris."

*

They were living in the flat in the Boulevard Soult, Ingrid and Rigaud, when she decided one afternoon to go back to the eighteenth arrondissement to talk to her father and tell him that she wanted to marry Rigaud as soon as possible.

She never read the papers. She didn't know that the "Missing" advertisement had appeared in an evening paper a few weeks earlier. She was shortly to be told of it by the *patron* of the hotel.

The snow had melted and it was so mild that you could go out without a coat. But there was still another month to go before the spring.

She had felt like walking, and she had gone down the boulevards towards Barbès-Rochechouart, which she had reached at about five. This time there was no curfew.

Ingrid had walked up and down outside the hotel, trying to find the words to justify her disappearance to her father. But they were all jumbled up in her head. She had walked round the block several times. Maybe he wasn't in his room at that hour. If he was still working at the Auteuil clinic, he'd be back for dinner. She'd wait for him in his room. She preferred that.

She went into the café. During the day, the hotel *patron* was behind the counter there. She asked him for the keys to rooms 3 and 5. He couldn't give them to her. Rooms 3 and 5 were occupied by other people.

He told her that very early one morning, about the middle of December, some policemen had gone up to look for her father in his room, and taken him away, he didn't know where.

*

I was lying on one of the twin beds, with the window wide open on to the Boulevard Soult. Night was falling. The phone rang. I thought for a moment that it was Annette, but how could she have got the number? I lifted the receiver. A metallic voice informed me that the line had been reconnected. Then I dialled our number at the Cité Véron. After two rings, I heard Annette's voice:

"Hallo? . . . Hallo?"

I said nothing.

"Hallo? . . . Is that you, Jean?"

I hung up.

Outside, I walked to the service station. The phone was still ringing in my head, a sound that had certainly not been heard in the flat since Ingrid and Rigaud had left it.

The concierge and the Kabyle in the blue dungarees were sitting on their chairs by the petrol pump and I shook hands with them.

"I've found you a bike," the Kabyle said.

And he pointed to a big red bike leaning against the office window. It didn't have racing handlebars.

"He had a lot of trouble finding it," said the concierge. "Because of the handlebars."

"Thank you very much," I said. "I wanted normal handlebars so as not to have to bend over. That way, I'd see the scenery."

"You won't be back too late?" the concierge asked.

"About midnight."

But I couldn't foresee my state of mind at that hour. No doubt I would feel like making a detour to the Cité Véron to see Annette, and – who knows? – staying at home.

*

There was a warm breeze – almost a sirocco – and a few dead leaves that it had blown off the trees were whirling around in the air. The first sign of autumn. I felt fine on the bike. I had been afraid I wouldn't be able to get up the slope in the Boulevard Mortier. But I did. It was easy. I didn't even need to pedal any more. A mysterious force carried me along. No cars. Silence. And even when the street lights became rather too far apart, I could see clearly, because of the full moon.

I hadn't imagined that it would be such a short way. To think that I'd been reluctant to leave the Porte Dorée for the Fieve Hotel, near the Buttes-Chaumont, as if it were the eve of a journey to Mongolia . . . They are very close, the Buttes-Chaumont, and, if I wanted to, in a few minutes I could get to 19, Rue de l'Atlas, where Ingrid lived with her father when she was a child. I had already reached the La Chapelle station, whose tracks and sheds I could just make out in the shadow below. Another few hundred metres along groups of sleeping blocks, and there was the Porte de Clignancourt. It was so very many years since I had been in this district that coming back to it that night I understood why all I had to do was let myself freewheel on the red bike: I was going back in time.

I started down the Boulevard Ornano and braked a little farther on, at the crossroads. I left the bike against the window of the chemist's. Nothing broke the silence. Except the water flowing along the gutter, murmuring like a fountain. That winter at the beginning of the sixties, when it had been so cold in Paris, we were living in an hotel in the Rue Championnet, whose name I have forgotten. A few steps in the street and I'd be outside it, but I preferred to carry straight on. In January that year Annette had had a favourable reply from the couture house and she had to go there one afternoon to be taken on for a trial period.

The previous day was a Sunday. It had been snowing. We went for a walk in the district. So one of us was beginning to work: we were becoming adult. We went into a café at the Porte de Clignancourt. We chose a table between two banquettes, right at the back, where a little jukebox had been stuck against the wall. That evening we wanted to go to the Ornano 43 cinema, but it was better to go to bed early so Annette would be on form the next day.

And now here I was arriving at that cinema, which had been turned into a shop. On the other side of the road, the hotel where Ingrid had lived with her father was no longer an hotel but a block like all the others. The café on the ground floor she had told me about no longer exists. One evening, she too had returned to this district, and for the first time she had felt a sense of emptiness.

Circumstances and settings are of no importance. One day this sense of emptiness and remorse submerges you. Then, like a tide, it ebbs and disappears. But in the end it returns in force, and she couldn't shake it off. Nor could I.

PATRICK MODIANO was born in a suburb of Paris and has published more than seventeen novels, including *Night Rounds* and *A Trace of Malice*, as well as the screenplay *Lacombe Lucien* (with Louis Malle). Another novel, *Missing Person*, is forthcoming from Godine. Mr. Modiano has been awarded a number of literary prizes, including the Grand Prix du Roman de l'Académie Française, the Prix de Monaco, and France's highest literary honor, the Prix Goncourt. *Honeymoon* is his fourth novel to be translated into English.

BARBARA WRIGHT is the translator of works by Raymond Queneau, Robert Pinget, Nathalie Sarraute, Alfred Jarry, Eugène Ionesco, and many of France's most challenging contemporary writers. She has twice been awarded the Scott-Moncrieff Prize.